DERWENT STEELE

THE PHANTOM SLAYER

Complete and Unabridged

LINFORD
Leicester

First published in Great Britain

First Linford Edition
published 2011

British Library CIP Data

Steele, Derwent.
  The phantom slayer. - -
  (Linford mystery library)
  1. Criminals- -Crimes against- -England- -
  London- -Fiction. 2. Jewel thieves- -Fiction.
  3. Detective and mystery stories.
  4. Large type books.
  I. Title II. Series
  823.9'12–dc22

  ISBN 978–1–4448–0638–0

Published by
F. A. Thorpe (Publishing)
Anstey, Leicestershire

Set by Words & Graphics Ltd.
Anstey, Leicestershire
Printed and bound in Great Britain by
T. J. International Ltd., Padstow, Cornwall

THE PHANTOM SLAYER

In London, criminals are being murdered — following lucrative crimes such as the jewel heist pulled off by Lew Steen. Like all the others, Steen receives a letter requesting a meeting — which must be attended — where the sender will buy the loot. However, the rock-bottom price on offer cannot be refused: those that refuse, die — horribly, from poison gas! Little wonder that the popular press labels their assailant as *The Phantom Slayer*. He has to be stopped — but how?

Books by Derwent Steele
in the Linford Mystery Library:

THE AVENGERS

1

The Car with the Green Light

The rain which had been threatening when Lew Steen boarded the bus at Piccadilly Circus had developed into a steady downpour, and when he descended at the station at Putney High Street he was glad of the forethought that had prompted him to bring his mackintosh. As he set off at a brisk pace in the direction of Putney Hill, the steep incline that leads up to the common, his mind was occupied by a number of varying and incongruous subjects, chief among which was the letter that had been the cause of bringing him out at such a late hour on this unpleasant night.

A clock struck twelve as he passed the policeman on point duty at the foot of the hill, and he increased his pace as he had a considerable distance to go before reaching his destination — the stretch of road

1

that runs across the heath between the Windmill and the Green Man.

Lew was a jewel thief, and the fact that the record department at Scotland Yard contained no reference concerning him testified to his ability. He smiled to himself in the darkness as his hands thrust in the deep pockets of his waterproof came in contact with a bulky packet. The Murley Diamonds were world famous and the newspapers had given full prominence to the robbery, and the cleverness with which it had been carried out — the reading of which on the following morning had given Lew a considerable amount of satisfaction, for he had spent a long time and no small amount of trouble in planning the theft, which had been negotiated without a hitch.

The diamonds, valued by the underwriters at close on a hundred thousand pounds, reposed in his pocket at that moment, and sent a warm glow of satisfaction through him as the packet flapped against his hip at every step. The proceeds would enable him to spend a lazy year — a year of luxury before he need turn his mind towards any fresh scheme to replenish his exchequer. His satisfaction, however, became somewhat damp as he remembered the letter and the reason for his midnight excursion to the lonely common and his rather thick brows drew together in a puzzled frown.

He had read the typewritten epistle that had reached him that morning so many times that every word was engraved in his memory. It was undated and unsigned, and ran:

★ ★ ★

'The night before last you obtained possession of the Murley Diamonds by burgling Lady Murley's flat in Park Lane. I wish to make you an offer for them. Be on the stretch of road that runs across Putney Heath between the Green Man and the Windmill at twelve thirty tonight. A car with a green light on the dashboard will approach you, stop it. If you fail to come, information implicating you with the robbery will reach Scotland

Yard by tomorrow morning. Bring the diamonds with you.'

* * *

That was all, and the receipt of it had given Lew much food for thought. Who was the unknown sender of the letter, and how had he become aware of Lew's connection with the robbery? After a lot of mental concentration he had come to the conclusion that it must have come from one of the many fences he was in the habit of dealing with, probably one of them had read the account of the theft in the papers and had recognised Lew's hand in the affair. There were only two men, he thought with a feeling of pride, who would have been capable of carrying out such a big pool, and he was one of them, the other, he remembered, was serving a five years' stretch at Dartmoor, so it was fairly easy to see how the writer of the letter had picked him out. But if it was someone with whom he had dealt before why hadn't he signed his name?

He was more puzzled than he cared to

admit, and just a trifle apprehensive. He didn't like the veiled threat conveyed in the last paragraph, in fact, but for that it was doubtful whether he would have kept the appointment at all. He had already approached old Linburg about the diamonds and was fairly confident of doing a quick deal with him, and he paid well — at least, well for a fence, who are notoriously mean.

Lew shivered as he reached the top of the hill and left the protection of the houses for the wind, which came across the open country and blew the rain in his face, was icy and found its way easily beneath the thin raincoat. He crossed the road and struck off diagonally across the heath. There was not a soul about, and the way ahead looked dark and uninviting. A vague sense of alarm suddenly passed over him but he thrust it aside and continued resolutely down the deserted roadway. In spite of the lamps which bordered the path at infrequent intervals it was uncomfortably dark, he found himself stumbling again and again into unsuspected puddles, and muttered curses on the head of the man who had brought him out of his cosy lodgings on such a night.

He had proceeded down the road for a considerable distance when he saw the blurred headlights of a car coming towards him. They drew wider apart as they drew nearer, and then, when some twenty yards distant suddenly glowed blindingly. He had already seen the tiny spark of green between them and stepped out into the roadway. The car slowed, the long, rain-streaming bonnet came past him and stopped, and from the dark interior of the coupe came a voice, low and harsh.

'Lew Steen?'

'That's me,' answered Lew, and strained his eyes to glimpse the figure inside.

He was just able to distinguish a muffled shape, a darker smudge of shadow against the blackness of the car's interior, but that was all.

'Come nearer,' said the voice, and Lew walked up to the open window.

A gloved hand rested on the edge and he saw the faint glint of light on what he took to be a pair of mica goggles that the unknown wore.

'Did you bring the diamonds?' the muffled voice continued, and Lew felt that he was being subjected to a close scrutiny.

'Well — ' he began hesitantly.

'If you didn't we're wasting time,' snarled the other, 'and you'll soon be doing it.'

'I did,' said Lew sullenly. 'Say, what's the idea? Who are you?'

'Never mind who I am,' answered the other shortly. 'How much do you want for those diamonds?'

'Well, they're worth — ' Lew began, but the unknown stopped him.

'I know what they're worth,' he snapped. 'I'll give you two hundred for them, cash.'

Lew Steen laughed, not a pleasant laugh.

'Know any more funny stories?' he sneered.

'You'll be wise if you accept my offer,' said the unseen man and his voice held a menace.

7

'I'd be insane if I did,' retorted Lew. 'I know where I can get at least ten thousand for them.'

'Then you won't deal?'

'No,' said Lew shaking his head.

'I'll give you one more chance,' growled the unknown. 'Two hundred cash.'

'We're wasting time,' answered Lew politely. 'Good night.'

He half turned away, and at the same instant the man in the car raised a gloved hand. The fingers grasped something short and squat. There was a muffled thud, and Lew Steen gave a choking gasp as he received the puff of poison gas full in his face. He was dead before his body reached the ground.

The unknown killer got down from the car and bent over the still form. His searching fingers quickly found the packet in the pocket of the dead jewel thief's mackintosh and he transferred it to his own heavy coat.

'You fool,' he muttered. 'If you'd only listened to reason you might be alive now.'

He returned to the car, removed the

gas mask that had concealed his face, the eyepieces of which Lew had taken for goggles. His foot sought for accelerator and the powerful engine hummed into brisker life. The car moved forward, gathered speed, and disappeared into the darkness of the night.

2

The Tragedy at Evesham Mansions —

On a foggy night towards the middle of November, some eight months since Lew Steen had met his death at the hand of an unknown murderer on the lonely road crossing Putney Heath, a taxi drew up outside a quiet house in Mecklinburg Square and a big man got wearily out, paid the driver and letting himself in with a latchkey entered a cosy room on the ground floor. A younger man who was sprawling on the settee in front of the fire half asleep, sat up as the other came in and yawned prodigiously.

'You're jolly late,' he remarked, glancing at the clock on the mantelpiece.

The big man nodded, removed his coat and hat, threw them on to a chair and sank into another near the fire with a sigh of relief.

'I called into the Yard on my way home

to see Kenton,' he replied, reaching towards a box of cigars that stood on a small table by his side. 'This latest murder is obviously by the same hand as the others.'

His secretary looked interested.

'The Phantom Slayer?' he asked, and his employer nodded.

'Yes,' he replied, carefully selecting and lighting a cigar. 'There's not the slightest doubt that it is the work of this mysterious man.' He blew out a cloud of fragrant smoke. 'As usual, the dead man was a well known criminal. They've got a record of him at the Yard and I expect you remember him, Simon Gold.'

'Simon Gold?' repeated the secretary wrinkling his brows. 'Yes, I believe I remember something about him. Didn't he specialise in raiding jewellers?'

'That's the fellow,' answered the other leaning back comfortably in his chair and puffing at his cigar. 'The cause of death was the same as in the other cases — some kind of poison gas.'

This big man who lay sprawled comfortably in the easy chair had at one time been attached to the Criminal Investigation Department at New Scotland Yard. His cleverness and acute reasoning powers had brought him early promotion, and then an uncle in the Colonies had died and left him an unexpected fortune. He had resigned from the Yard but had continued to interest himself in crime, building up a respectable practice as a private investigator.

John Blackmore was the last court of appeal. To him came many clients, rich and poor, and since his work was his hobby and his unexpected fortune had rendered him independent, he was able to pick and choose just those cases which supplied him with the maximum of interest. Together with his secretary, Harry Cartwright, he had probed into many strange businesses, and solved quite a number of mysteries which Scotland Yard had declared unsolvable.

Since the early hours of that morning, when a telephone message from Inspector Kenton had brought him from his bed soon after dawn, he had been out.

The body of an unknown man had been found stone dead by the police patrol on the lonely stretch of road crossing Wimbledon Common, and Kenton had asked Blackmore to accompany him on his investigations. There had been no difficulty in identifying the body, for Simon Gold had served no less than three sentences, and his record took up a considerable space in one of the long, shallow drawers with which a certain room in Scotland Yard is lined. The 'Gold' murder was the latest in a series of inexplicable crimes of the same stamp that had been baffling the police for some time past. The first victim having been a jewel thief named Lew Steen, whose dead body had been found in the vicinity of Putney Heath some eight months previously. At varying intervals after that five other murders had taken place in lonely parts of London and the suburbs, and in every case the victim had proved, upon investigation, to be a well known crook. The cause of death was the same in each instance — as the medical evidence testified — some highly poisonous form of gas, having as its base hydrocyanic acid, had been used by the unknown murderer.

It was partly for this reason and partly because of the mystery underlying the motive of the series of fatalities that caused George Mellish, crime reporter of the *Megaphone* to give the man responsible the name of the 'Phantom Slayer' — a name which had remained since the first glaring headlines had splashed it across the front of his paper.

Detective Inspector Kenton had been put in charge of the case following the third murder, after a heated interview with the disgruntled Assistant Commissioner and had come to John Blackmore for help and to investigate the crime.

The private investigator had been working on the strange affair for several months, and although he had done his utmost, so far he had been unable to unearth the slightest clue that was likely to lead to the identity of the mysterious killer. One thing, however, he had discovered, and that was that in every case the dead criminal had, just prior to his murder perpetrated a large robbery, the proceeds of which had completely disappeared. A search of the belongings of two of the murdered men resulted in the finding of two letters, both typewritten and unsigned, and both making appointments for the same night and at the place where the bodies of the recipients had been found. The wording in each letter was the same, varying only as regards the time and place of the appointment.

The discovery of these letters had caused Blackmore to form a theory which at least suggested the motive behind the apparently reasonless series of crime. They demanded that the recipient should bring with him the proceeds of the particular robbery in which he had been concerned, and ended with the threat that failure to keep the appointment would result in proof of his connection with the affair being sent at once to Scotland Yard. Apparently a new type of criminal had appeared and his method of working was fairly obvious. He was evidently out to make money with as little risk to himself as possible, waiting until some burglary had been committed, large enough to make it worth his while, he discovered by some means or other the identity of the criminal responsible, immediately communicated with him, making an appointment that the crook concerned was forced to keep under threat of exposure to the police. At the interview he made a ridiculously small offer for the proceeds of the robbery and if this was refused killed the unfortunate crook with some kind of poison gas apparatus and took the swag. By this means he was able to reap the profits while others did the work and took the risk. It was a clever scheme and up till the present appeared to have worked remarkably well.

This was John Blackmore's theory and it had been substantiated by the story of two jewel thieves who had been arrested for the burglary of a West End jewellers, and the robbery of a flat respectively. On being questioned they had admitted to each receiving one of the 'Phantom

Slayer's' letters. They had kept the appointment, the mysterious writer arriving in a closed car, his face concealed by a rubber mask with mica eyepieces, and they had sold the jewellery they had secured for little more than a song, because knowing what had happened in the other cases they had been afraid for their lives to do otherwise.

The advent of the 'Phantom Slayer' had caused something of a panic in the underworld. His possible identity was discussed nightly in mean lodging houses and luxurious flats, by down-at-heel loafers lounging round the bars of obscure public houses and immaculately dressed men in glittering night clubs.

John Blackmore had listened to many conjectures while in various disguises he had spent night after night in the less known haunts of crime, in the hope of lighting on some chance word that would lead him to the unknown murderer. One thing was evident, the underworld regarded the 'Phantom Slayer' as a menace to themselves, and the crooks, from the highest to the lowest, were as keen to get him as were the police.

'Did you discover anything fresh today?' asked Cartwright, after Blackmore had sat smoking for some time in silence.

His employer shook his head wearily.

'Nothing,' he replied. 'As in all the other cases, he's been too clever for us. Whoever he is he's got brains.'

'What beats me,' said the secretary, 'is how on earth he knows who to send these letters to. How can he be certain that he's not making an appointment with the wrong man?'

Blackmore stared thoughtfully at the end of his cigar.

'I don't quite understand that myself,' he replied. 'The only explanation is that he must be getting some inside information from somewhere, for as far as we know he never has made a mistake up to now.' He rose to his feet with a sigh and flicked the ash from his cigar into the fireplace. 'It's useless trying to conjecture anything until we can find a concrete clue to work on,' he remarked. 'Up to the present he has been too clever to leave anything behind him that would give us the slightest inkling to his identity, but he's bound to make a mistake sooner or later, they all do, and the only thing is to wait and watch. We can do nothing more.' He yawned and stretched himself. 'I think I'll go to bed,' he continued. 'I've had a pretty hard day, and I've got an early session with Kenton in the morning.'

Cartwright had opened his mouth to reply when the telephone rang shrilly. John Blackmore glanced at the clock.

'Who the devil can that be?' he muttered, crossing over to the instrument.

Lifting the receiver from the hook he placed it to his ear. There was a confused buzzing for a moment and then a voice came over the wire.

'Is that Mr. Blackmore?'

'Speaking,' answered the private investigator, 'who's that?'

'I want to see you immediately,' was the hurried reply. 'Can you come at once to 4, Evesham Mansions? I've something important to tell you. It's about the 'Phantom Slayer.''

'Who are you?' broke in Blackmore, a

note of excitement creeping into his voice.

'I can't say any more now,' the caller sounded faint and far away. 'Come quickly.'

'But — ' began Blackmore, when he heard a click, the unknown had rung off.

'Who was it?' asked Cartwright, who had been listening curiously.

'I don't know,' answered John. 'Someone who is anxious to tell me something about the 'Phantom Slayer'.' He briefly related the conversation. 'It was a man's voice,' he concluded. 'Get your coat on, we'll go round and see.'

All trace of tiredness had vanished from his face and manner, and he was already struggling into his overcoat.

A taxi was crawling by as they opened the front door, and Blackmore hailed it. When they reached the West End they found that the theatre traffic had long since ceased and the streets were practically deserted, so that in an incredibly short space of time they arrived at their destination.

Evesham Mansions proved to be a large

block of flats in a quiet street in Maida Vale, and paying off the driver of the cab, Blackmore ran swiftly up the half-a-dozen steps that led to the darkened entrance. Most of the inhabitants had apparently gone to bed for there were no lights to be seen anywhere. Number four was on the third floor and as John reached the head of the stairs he saw that this was an exception for a glimmer of light showed through the frosted glass panel of the door. There was a brass bell push to the right of the jamb, and raising his hand he pressed the little ivory button. He heard the shrill buzz of the electric bell from inside and waited expectantly, but all was silent. He glanced at the door of the adjoining flat, number five, while he waited and saw that it was in darkness. After a moment or two he rang again.

'Doesn't seem as if there's anyone in,' whispered Cartwright at his elbow.

Blackmore frowned.

'I don't like the look of things,' he muttered shaking his head.

There was no reply to his second ring, and he bent down, and lifting the flap of the letter box peered in. The light came from a half opened door at the end of the tiny hall, but there was not the slightest sound or movement in the flat. Suddenly he sniffed, a faint, not unpleasant odour had come to his nostrils, an odour that was curiously reminiscent of a hospital ward. Blackmore's face set in a hard mask as he straightened up.

'There's something wrong here,' he said gently. 'I'm going to break open the door.'

He searched in an inside pocket and presently withdrew a strangely shaped little instrument of hardened steel. For a few moments he worked on the lock, and then suddenly there came a sharp click, and the door swung open. He stepped into the dimly lit hall followed by Cartwright. The peculiar smell was more pungent. Closing the door behind them they crossed the little passage and threw wide the partly open door at the end.

On the threshold Blackmore stopped with an exclamation of alarm.

The room beyond was comfortably furnished as a sitting room. Sprawling face downwards on the floor was the figure of a man. In two strides Blackmore was beside the still form, and stooping turned it gently over. One glance was sufficient to show him that the man was dead, at the same instant he realised the significance of the curious chemical like odour which filled the place, for the man on the floor had died from the effects of the poison gas used by the 'Phantom Slayer.'

3

The Plaster Chips

John Blackmore straightened up and turned to his secretary who was standing dumb with astonishment, in the doorway.

'Go and fetch a doctor,' he ordered sharply, 'and if you see a constable ask him to notify the nearest police station.'

'But — ' began Cartwright, when his employer stopped him with a quick gesture.

'Don't wait to ask questions,' he snapped. 'Hurry!' And Cartwright, who knew him in these moods hastened to obey.

Left alone, Blackmore stood for some seconds surveying the motionless form of the man on the floor, and there was a hard, steely glint in his eyes. This man, whoever he was, and as far as he knew he had never seen him before in his life, had something of vital importance to communicate concerning the 'Phantom Slayer,' hence the urgency of his telephone message. What had been that something? Had he discovered the unknown murderer's identity, and had the 'Phantom Slayer,' aware of the fact, killed him to prevent his information reaching the police? It seemed beyond his solution. The murderer must have worked quickly, for little more than a quarter of an hour had passed from the time Blackmore had received the message and his arrival at the flat. He remembered the dead man's words.

'I can't say any more now,' and the hurried way he had rung off.

It seemed almost as if he had suddenly become aware that he was being over-heard.

Still thinking, Blackmore allowed his eyes to travel slowly round the room. It was a medium sized apartment, furnished half as a sitting room and half as a study. A table, on which stood the remains of a meal, was drawn up beside an easy chair by the fireplace, in which a gas fire, turned half down, burned steadily. Opposite the fireplace was a large window, the curtains closely drawn. A blank wall faced the door by which he and Cartwright had entered and against this was set a bureau desk which was shut. Blackmore walked over to the window and moved the curtains. As he had expected it overlooked the street. Raising the lower sash he looked out. A thirty foot drop ran sheer to the narrow strip of garden that divided the block of flats from the pavement.

John peered from side to side, seeking some means by which anyone could have gained egress that way, but there was not even a drain pipe and he mentally ruled out the window as a possible means of entrance to the flat. The murderer of the unknown man on the floor had got in somehow, and Blackmore was certain that it had not been by way of the front door — unless the person, whoever it was, possessed a key. The idea set up a new train of thought and he closed the window and walked over to the door. Passing out into the tiny lobby he found the light switch and pressed it down.

The little hall was plainly furnished

with a coat stand and two chairs. A mackintosh hung on one of the pegs and he passed his hand slowly over its shiny surface. It was still damp. He noted the fact, storing it up in the recesses of his memory for future reference. It seemed unimportant at the moment, but it was his habit to discard nothing, however trivial, and it was this passion for detail that had placed him in the front rank of his profession.

There were two other doors leading out of the hall, and opening the first of these Blackmore discovered himself in a bedroom. The window, outside of which ran an iron fire escape was latched and a close scrutiny assured him that it had not been opened for some time. He made a quick search of the room, but beyond the fact that a thin layer of dust had settled over every article of furniture he found nothing of interest.

The dust puzzled him. It was obvious that the room had not been used — at least, not for several days. Where then had the dead man slept? Perhaps there was another bedroom. Going back to the hall he tried the other door. It led into a fairly spacious kitchen. Here again he found a similar layer of dust. The china on the dresser was covered with it, as also was a row of cooking utensils on a shelf above a little gas stove. A frying pan and a little saucepan had, however, been recently used, and a pile of dirty crockery littered the sink. Apart from the room he had first entered the whole place appeared unused and neglected. He crossed over to the window and found that this too was latched, and the hasp rusted. It had evidently not been opened for weeks.

A door on the left of the fireplace caught his eyes and looking in he saw that the narrow room beyond was a bathroom, he saw also that it must have been a considerable time since it was used for the purpose it had been intended, for the bottom of the bath was covered with debris and red with rust where the white enamel had chipped off. John Blackmore's brows drew together in a frown and he stood at the door for several seconds rubbing his chin thoughtfully.

He was frankly puzzled, it was obvious

from the state of the flat that no one had actually been living there, and yet the sitting room presented every indication of having been occupied, and the kitchen showed that several meals had recently been cooked. But that apparently was the only room the dead man had used. Still turning this problem over in his mind Blackmore made his way back to the hall, and spent some time on a close examination of the front door, and at the end of his scrutiny he was convinced that the lock had not been forced prior to his own opening of the door. Had it been, he himself would never have been able to have picked it so easily as he had. How then had the unknown murderer got in? Blackmore had assured himself that it was not by any of the windows, the only possible one was that of the bedroom which opened on to the fire escape, and a glance at the fastening had told him that it had not been touched. The person, whoever it was, responsible for the death of the man in the sitting room must have entered by the front door and in that case, unless he had been admitted by the dead man himself, it seemed fairly obvious to conclude he had possessed a key.

Having reached this supposition John was about to return to the sitting room when the sound of footsteps on the stone stairway outside made him pause. They stopped at the door and a second later the bell rang, echoing shrilly in the silent flat. Blackmore opened the door and found that Cartwright had returned, accompanied by a constable and a short dark man who had evidently dressed himself hurriedly, for the collar of a pyjama jacket showed beneath the overcoat he wore. They stepped into the hall and Blackmore closed the door behind them.

'This is Doctor Lake' said the secretary, introducing the man in the overcoat. 'He lives in the next block. I've explained what has happened.'

'An extraordinary affair, Mr. Blackmore,' said the little doctor. 'There's no doubt about the man being dead, I suppose?'

Blackmore shook his head, and led the way towards the sitting room.

'Not the slightest, I'm afraid,' he answered. 'You can see for yourself.' He indicated the small figure prone on the floor and the doctor knelt down beside it.

'Did you get through to the station?' said Blackmore turning to the constable who was standing by his side.

'Yes, sir,' answered the man. 'I 'phoned from the call box at the end of the street directly your secretary told me what had happened. Inspector Tillit is coming up at once.'

The doctor looked up from his brief examination of the body as the policeman finished speaking.

'He's stone dead,' he said in a low voice. 'Some kind of poison gas has been used, though I can't tell you offhand what it was, or how it was administered. How did you come to find it?'

Blackmore explained in a few sentences, and at the mention of the 'Phantom Slayer' the doctor pursed his lips and frowned.

'So he's connected with the affair, is he?' he remarked. 'I've read a lot about that fellow in the papers.'

'I hope the next you read will be an account of his trial,' said Blackmore grimly.

He looked down at the white, staring face of the man on the floor. The 'Phantom Slayer' had added another victim to the already long list of his crimes, and John made a mental vow that he would never rest until he had run the man to earth and sent him to the gallows. Cartwright, who was standing at his elbow broke in on his thoughts.

'Have you discovered who this chap was?' he asked.

His employer shook his head.

'No,' he replied. 'I haven't searched the body yet. There will probably be some letters or documents in his pockets that can tell us.'

He knelt down and carefully, so as not to disturb the position in which the dead man lay, for the police would want to take photographs, he proceeded to examine the clothing. There was nothing, not the smallest scrap of paper, likely to help in identifying him. A cigarette case half full of Virginia cigarettes, a box of matches, a bunch of keys and a gold watch were all the pockets yielded. He put these back exactly where he had found them and rose to his feet. The doctor, waiting over by the door addressed him as he did so.

'You won't want me any more, will you?' he asked. 'I'll write out my report and send it to the station in the morning, I haven't had very much sleep lately and I've got a fairly heavy day tomorrow.'

'No, there's nothing to keep you, Doctor,' answered Blackmore, and the little man with a sigh of relief and a hurried good night left them.

When he had gone John looked across at the desk over by the opposite wall.

'There may be something there that will give us a clue to the man's identity,' he said, half to Cartwright and half to himself, and was about to walk over to it when an exclamation from his secretary stopped him.

While John had been talking to the doctor Cartwright had been looking round the room and his eyes had suddenly become attracted by something white that lay on the stained portion of floor between the carpet and the wall beside the fireplace. It resembled powdered chalk.

'What is it?' Blackmore paused on his way to the desk to ask the question.

'Over there.' His secretary pointed to a place on the floor to the left of the fireplace. 'There's some kind of white stuff, I've only just seen it.'

Blackmore went over to the wall and bent down. Close up by the skirting board was a little heap of white powder. He picked some of it up in his fingers and found that intermingled with it were a number of tiny wood shavings.

'What is it?' asked Cartwright curiously staring at the particles that lay in his employer's palm.

'Plaster,' answered Blackmore shortly and began to examine the wall. A second later he turned to his secretary, his eyes gleaming with suppressed excitement.

'There's a hole here — by the side of this picture.'

'A hole?' The constable who had been watching interestedly came over.

'Yes,' said John. 'It's been bored right

through the wall.' He bent closer and applied his eye to the tiny aperture, and Cartwright heard his breath hiss sharply as he drew it in. For a moment he remained there, and then straightened up. 'You can see into the sitting room of the next flat,' he announced. 'The lights are on but it appears to be empty.'

Cartwright looked at him in astonishment.

'What in the world — ' he began, but Blackmore cut him short.

'I'm going to have a look at the adjoining flat, it should prove interesting. Stay here will you, Officer? and you come with me.'

With his secretary at his heel he hurried into the hall and opening the front door stepped out into the landing. As he was about to approach the door of number five it was suddenly thrown violently open and a man rushed out. He cannoned into Blackmore, sending him reeling against Cartwright and before either of them could recover their balance the sound of his clattering footsteps on the stone stairs was fading in the distance.

'After him,' snapped Blackmore, struggling to his feet. 'Don't let him get away if you can help it.'

The secretary needed no second bidding, and almost before the words had left Blackmore's lips he was speeding down the stairs in the wake of the stranger. The noise had brought the constable out to see what was the matter.

'A man?' he exclaimed when Blackmore told him the cause of the racket. 'What was he like?'

'I couldn't tell you,' answered John a trifle impatiently. 'The whole thing happened so suddenly I was completely taken by surprise. So far as I could see he had some kind of handkerchief tied round the lower part of his face.'

He surveyed the open door of number five.

'I'm going in to have a look round, I think the best thing you can do is to stay here.'

The hall, which he guessed was a replica of the one next door since it ran parallel, was in complete darkness, but as he stepped across the threshold he saw a narrow pencil of light that streamed from under the door of the sitting room.

Blackmore stopped halfway down the passage and listened but there was not a sound, and after a few seconds' pause he proceeded on towards the door at the end. Grasping the handle he turned it quickly and flung the door wide open. The room was empty. He was on the point of entering when a sound reached his ears, and caused him to turn sharply and listen. There was a faint creak, and it seemed to come from the hall. It was no longer dark there for the light from the sitting room streamed through the open door and illumined every corner. Again he heard the creaking sound and this time he located it. It came from a door that was partly open and corresponded to the bedroom door of the adjoining flat. John crossed to it. The room beyond was in darkness and hesitating for the fraction of a second, he pushed the door open and feeling for the light switch pressed it down.

The sudden blaze of light revealed a comfortably furnished bedroom. It also revealed something else. On the bed, his ankles and wrists securely bound and a gag in his mouth, lay the figure of a man, and as he saw him John Blackmore gave a cry of surprise for the man was George Mellish, star crime reporter of the *Megaphone*.

4

George Mellish's Story

It took Blackmore but a few moments to cut the cords that bound Mellish and remove the gag from his mouth.

'How in God's name did you get like this?' he asked as the reporter struggled to a sitting position and rubbed his chafed wrists.

'I was attacked,' replied Mellish in a weak voice.

He looked dazed and shaken, and John quickly discovered the cause when he saw the lump on the back of the man's head.

'Tell me exactly what happened,' he said.

Mellish passed a trembling hand across his forehead.

'There's very little to tell,' he answered huskily for the gag had been tied tightly and his tongue and lips were swollen. 'I was sitting in the other room writing — '

'Do you live here?' interrupted Blackmore.

The reporter nodded, and winced at the pain the movement cost him.

'Yes.' He leaned back against the foot of the bed. 'As I said, I was writing at my desk with my back to the door when a slight sound caused me to turn round. I was just in time to see a tall man in a long black overcoat enter the room. It was the click of the door handle that possibly disturbed me. He was wearing a handkerchief over the lower part of his face so that I couldn't tell what he was like. I half rose from my chair but before I could do anything the man sprang at me. Something descended on the back of my head and I don't remember any more until I recovered consciousness to find myself lying on the bed as you saw me.'

'Is that all?' asked John disappointedly.

'That's all,' said Mellish.

'And there was nothing by which you would be able to recognise the man again?'

'Absolutely nothing.'

Blackmore pursed his lips thoughtfully.

'I suppose you know there's no reason for this attack?' he queried.

'None,' replied the reporter. 'I'm completely mystified.'

John was silent for a moment.

'Who occupies the flat next door?' he asked suddenly.

Mellish looked surprised.

'You mean number four?' he enquired.

Blackmore nodded.

'I really don't know. It's been empty for some time. The original tenant went abroad and sold his furniture to the landlord, I believe. A man called Dowling took it about three weeks ago, but I couldn't be sure. If anyone has been living there I've never seen him.'

'You've never seen him?' echoed John incredulously.

'No.' Mellish shook his head. 'I've heard him of course — several times — but only at night.'

'D'you mean late at night?' asked Blackmore.

'I used to hear his front door close about eleven thirty — I think he invariably went out at the time.'

41

'What time did he come in?' said John.

'Well, it's a curious thing,' answered the reporter, 'but to tell you the truth I never heard him come back. He must have done so, naturally, but it must have been very late. Why all these questions?'

'Because Dowling, or whatever his name is, was murdered this evening, in his sitting room,' replied John Blackmore grimly.

'Murdered! Good God!' Mellish looked horror stricken. 'When was this?'

'About an hour ago, as near as I can tell,' said the private investigator. 'Did you hear any sounds in the next flat?'

'Not a sound,' declared Mellish. 'But then he was always very quiet.'

Blackmore stood for a moment in silence stroking his chin thoughtfully.

'I wonder how the man who attacked you got in,' he remarked at length, and without waiting for a reply he walked across to the window and pulled aside the heavy curtains that hung over it. A brief examination of the catch told him all he wanted to know. There was a deep scratch in the brass and it was fresh. He pushed up the lower sash and leaned out. An iron fire escape ran close beside the window. Taking an electric torch from his pocket he played a shaft of light on the sill. Plainly to be seen were the marks of muddy footprints.

'There's not much doubt about the way he came,' he said closing the window.

'Do you think he was responsible for the crime next door?' asked Mellish; rising unsteadily to his feet by the aid of the bedrail.

'I think it's more than likely,' answered Blackmore, 'seeing that the murder was undoubtedly committed from inside this flat.'

The reporter stared at him in blank amazement.

'Committed from here?' he repeated slowly. 'How?'

'Come into the sitting room and I'll show you,' said John.

Mellish followed him, staggering slightly, into the little hall. Blackmore walked to the door at the end, flung it open. He uttered a little exclamation as he did so and darted forward.

'What is it?' cried the reporter quickly, as Blackmore stooped and picked something up from the centre of the floor.

John made no reply but carried his find over to the electric light. It was a squat, curiously shaped pistol, and he examined it carefully. It was empty but had evidently been made to fire gas cartridges. Blackmore had seen something similar before, in America, though not quite the same pattern.

'Unless I'm greatly mistaken,' he murmured, 'it's the weapon that was used to kill Dowling.'

Mellish had crossed to his side and was gazing at the pistol curiously.

'I've never seen anything that shape before,' he said.

John shook his head.

'I don't suppose you have,' he answered with a faint smile. 'This is a gas pistol.'

'What do you mean?' asked the reporter.

'Instead of firing bullets,' explained Blackmore, 'it ejects a puff of poison gas which is compressed at high pressure in the cartridge. The principle is somewhat similar to that used in the making of soda water in a 'Sparklet' syphon.'

Mellish looked at the weapon in horrified amazement.

'And you say that it was used to kill the man next door,' he said incredulously and in a low voice.

'Without a doubt,' replied John.

His eyes had been travelling round the room as he was speaking, and now they came to rest on a portion of the wall beside the fireplace. He crossed swiftly over and looked at the place and turned and beckoned Mellish.

'That's how it was done,' he remarked and pointed.

The reporter's eyes opened wide as he saw the hole.

'The murderer bored through the wall,' John continued, 'and by some means or other persuaded Dowling to come across to the aperture, then he discharged the pistol in his face.'

'But why go to all that trouble?' asked the reporter, in a perplexed tone.

John frowned.

'I can't tell you at the moment,' he

replied. 'It does seem rather unnecessary when he could just have easily have broken into the other flat. I suppose there was a purpose in it, although we can't see one at present. The 'Phantom Slayer' doesn't usually do things without a good reason.'

'The 'Phantom Slayer'?' Mellish gasped the name breathlessly. 'You're not suggesting that he's got anything to do with this?'

'I'm doing more than suggesting,' answered Blackmore. 'I'm sure of it.' He gave the reporter a brief account of the telephone message that had brought him to the flat. 'Somehow or other this fellow Dowling discovered something about the 'Slayer',' he concluded, 'and he became aware of the fact and killed him to prevent his making any statement to me.'

'Then the man who attacked me — he must have been the 'Phantom Slayer' himself,' exclaimed the reporter aghast.

'In all probability he was,' replied Blackmore. 'So far as we know he works alone, that's one of the principal reasons why he's never been caught. He trusts no one and therefore no one can squeal.'

He set to work on a quick but thorough examination of the room. Under an easy chair by the hearth he discovered a brace and bit — obviously the instrument that had been used to bore the hole in the wall. Traces of wood and plaster still remained in the worm of the screw. He picked it up carefully by the steel and laid it on a sheet of paper on the desk. There was just a chance that the handle might yield prints. He continued his search, and although he didn't overlook a square inch of space nothing else in the nature of a clue came to light. He had just finished when Cartwright came back.

'I lost him,' said the secretary bitterly. 'He disappeared, running like the wind down a side turning, and when I got up to it there was not a sign of him.'

'Never mind, it can't be helped.' Blackmore straightened up. 'I was afraid he had too big a start.' He glanced keenly round the little sitting room. 'I don't think there's anything more to be learned here, we'll go back to the other flat.'

They reached the landing just as the

inspector and another constable were ascending the stairs.

Inspector Heel was a tall, thin man, and he touched his hat on seeing Blackmore.

'I got your message, sir,' he said. 'What's all the trouble here? Constable Rawlings didn't give me any details except that a man had been killed.'

John took him into the hall of Dowling's flat and in a few sentences explained what had occurred.

'The 'Phantom Slayer,' eh,' exclaimed Heel. 'It seems an extraordinary business altogether. Have you found any clue?'

Blackmore shook his head.

'No,' he replied. 'I think you had better take charge of the brace and bit, they'll want it at the Yard to test for fingerprints, though I should think, personally, that he was clever enough to have worn gloves.' He turned to Mellish. 'Can you remember whether the man who attacked you wore gloves or not?' he asked.

The reporter wrinkled his forehead in thought.

'I couldn't be certain,' he replied

candidly, after a slight pause. 'The whole thing was so sudden and took me so completely by surprise that it would be impossible for me to give you any detailed description of his appearance.'

The inspector sent one of the policemen to fetch the brace, instructing him to avoid touching the handle, and then he followed John into the room of death.

'I suppose you've already searched the body?' he enquired, as he stood looking down at the silent form.

'Yes,' said Blackmore, 'but there's nothing of any interest.'

He walked over to the bureau desk and tried the lid. It was unlocked and raising the flap he looked inside. The pigeon holes were full of neatly packed papers. While the inspector questioned Mellish concerning his mysterious visitor, Blackmore, with Cartwright's assistance, began to search the papers in the desk. Most of them were old letters and documents belonging to the previous tenant, but presently they came to a few stray papers thrust aside in a shallow drawer and Blackmore caught sight of the address on an envelope and gave vent to a slight involuntary exclamation.

'What is it?' asked his secretary eagerly.

John showed him the letter. The name on the envelope was James Falkner, and it was addressed to the *Daily Call*, Fleet Street, E.C.4.

'What have you found?' enquired Inspector Heel, breaking off his conversation with Mellish and hurrying over.

'I think I've discovered an important clue,' said John. 'The identity of the murdered man.'

'I thought his name was Dowling,' began the inspector when Blackmore interrupted him.

'I'm sure that was an alias,' he said. 'This I'm convinced is his real name.'

The inspector looked at the superscription on the envelope and pursed his rather thin lips.

'Falkner!' he said, but got no further, for Mellish broke in with a cry.

'Good God! Not James Falkner?' he exclaimed, and Blackmore nodded. 'Why he's the special crime reporter on the staff of the *Daily Call*. It can't be Falkner.'

'Do you know him well?' asked Blackmore. 'I've heard of him, of course, but I never met him.'

'I know him almost as well as I know you,' said the reporter.

'Then would you mind looking at the body and telling us if you can identify it?' said the inspector.

The face of the murdered man had been turned away from that part of the room in which Mellish had been standing, and the reporter had avoided going nearer. Now, at the inspector's request he stepped over and bent down.

'Yes, it's Falkner right enough,' he said after a second with a little catch in his breath. 'Poor old Jim.'

The inspector looked at Blackmore with a puzzled expression on his face.

'This is extraordinary,' he ejaculated. 'Why on earth should this man have been living here under an assumed name?'

John rubbed his chin thoughtfully.

'There's every indication,' he replied slowly, 'that he never lived here at all.'

'Never lived here?' The inspector's face was almost comical in its dismay.

Blackmore inclined his head.

'He used to come here, but I'm prepared to swear that he never slept here,' he answered. 'The state of the other rooms are conclusive proof of that. And the bed has not been used for a considerable time.'

'Then what did he come here at all for?' demanded Heel.

Blackmore shrugged his shoulders.

'I can't tell you that,' he said. 'Possibly we might learn something further if we rang up the offices of the *Daily Call*. They are bound to know a good deal more about his movements.'

The telephone stood on a small table in one corner, and going over to the instrument as he spoke, John lifted the receiver. There was no sound from the earpiece. The usual 'hum' was absent.

'The line's dead,' he remarked as he hung up the black cylinder. 'It's probably been cut somewhere.'

They traced the wire, it ran under the door, along the hall and out into the landing, through a hole by the side of the fanlight. Close to the front door it had been neatly severed.

'That's why his voice faded away while he was speaking to me,' said Blackmore, looking at the frayed strands. 'Can you connect up these ends, Cartwright?'

The secretary nodded. By the aid of a chair he was able to reach the place and in a few minutes had succeeded in executing a rough repair.

'What's the number of the *Daily Call's* office?' asked Blackmore turning to Mellish, when it was done.

The reporter told him, and he asked to be put through. A little later he was talking to the News editor. The conversation was a fairly long one, and when he had finished John turned to the others.

'Falkner received a special commission from the *Daily Call* people about a month ago to devote all his time to tracking down the 'Phantom Slayer',' he announced, hanging up the receiver. 'Since that time they haven't seen him. He completely disappeared, and with the exception of one or two brief notes they heard nothing from him. The last message came from him yesterday, and stated that he was following up a clue, and hoped shortly to make a sensational statement. That's all.'

'Didn't they know he was occupying this flat?' asked Mellish.

'They didn't know where he was,' replied Blackmore, 'and were horrified when I told them he was dead. In some ways the mystery's a little clearer, though I can't understand why Falkner should have taken up his abode in this place. Particularly as it's obvious that he only spent part of his time here.'

'It certainly is peculiar,' said Mellish, with knitted brows. 'Wonder what his object could have been?'

Blackmore shook his head.

'It's impossible to conjecture at the moment,' he answered absently.

He let his eyes travel slowly round the room, and Cartwright, who was watching him, saw that far away introspective look that always betokened that his employer was deep in thought. There was a pause, and then with a sudden movement of his shoulders Blackmore roused himself.

'I think we may as well be getting back home,' he remarked to his secretary.

'I must go down to the *Megaphone*,' said Mellish, 'and write up an account of the affair. You won't want me any more?' He addressed the inspector.

'No,' replied Heel. 'Of course you'll be wanted at the inquest, I suppose I can always find you at your flat.'

'Either there or at the offices of the paper,' answered the reporter, and said good night to Blackmore and Cartwright and took his leave.

John remained talking for a few moments to the inspector and then leaving the officer in charge, he called his secretary and together they made their way down the stone stairway to the street. As they emerged from the entrance Cartwright, who was a little ahead, suddenly caught sight of something which glistened in the rays of the street lamp outside. It was lying at the base of one of the bushes with which the narrow belt of gardens surrounding the building was filled. He stooped and picked it up. It was a gold wrist watch.

'Look at this,' he cried excitedly, and held his find out to Blackmore.

John took it, and carrying it out to the pavement examined it carefully under the lamp. The suede strap that fastened the watch to the wrist was worn thin near the buckle and had snapped.

'D'you think it was dropped by the man who ran away?' asked Cartwright, at his employer's elbow.

'Possible,' replied Blackmore. 'In fact I should say probable, since it was lying in a conspicuous position, for if it had been there long it would have undoubtedly been seen by someone entering or leaving the flat.'

He turned the tiny piece of jewellery about in his hand.

'If it did belong to the man who had attacked Mellish it should provide us with a distinct clue. He held the watch closer to the light, and peered intently at the face. 'It was manufactured by a British firm,' he continued after a moment's inspection. 'Beal and Son, Cannon Street. The name is printed on the dial, just over the minute hand. We'll get in touch with them first thing in the morning.'

With his nail he prised open the back,

on the thin gold above the Hall Mark was stamped a number, 10237. John pointed it out to his secretary.

'They are certain to have a record in their sales book of the jeweller to whom this watch was supplied,' he said, 'and if we can find them they may be able to remember who bought it.'

He put the watch in his pocket and looked round for a taxi, but the hour was late and the street deserted.

'I'm afraid we shall have to walk,' he went on after a moment or two. 'We may be able to pick up a cab on the way.'

They set off at a brisk pace. The fog which had been fairly thick earlier in the evening had disappeared, and a thin drizzle of rain had taken its place, which made walking anything but pleasant.

'Do you think the man who broke into Mellish's flat was the 'Phantom Slayer' himself?' asked Cartwright as they strode along.

'Everything seems to point to it,' replied John. 'It was undoubtedly the 'Phantom Slayer' who killed poor Falkner, the method by which the murder was committed proves that.'

'But why should he have gone to the trouble and risk of breaking into Mellish's flat?' said Harry in a puzzled tone. 'It seems to me that it would have been far easier if he had gone direct to Falkner.'

'I agree with you,' answered Blackmore. 'I must confess that there are several features about the case that puzzle me, and the unnecessary trouble he appears to have gone to is the most inexplicable. So far as I can reason it out the sequence of his end must run something like this. Falkner is, we know, instructed by the *Daily Call* people to devote his time to tracking down the 'Phantom Slayer,' for some reason or other, which we do not know at present, he considered it necessary to drop his own identity and assume the name of Dowling for the purpose of taking a furnished flat in Evesham Mansions. He doesn't live there but appears to use it as a kind of temporary headquarters. In some way, which also we do not know, he manages to discover vital information concerning the 'Phantom Slayer.' The unknown murderer learns of this, and when Falkner is in the act of ringing me up he cuts the telephone wire outside the door of the flat — I mistook the noise for Falkner's ringing off — goes round to the back, enters Mellish's flat by way of the fire escape and the bedroom window, overpowers Mellish, and boring a hole through the wall entices Falkner over to the aperture, and then killed him by discharging the contents of this poison gas pistol in his face. Now, although Falkner must have known that someone cut the telephone wire, and although it must have taken a considerable time for the 'Phantom Slayer' to have got into Mellish's flat, Falkner, apparently, meanwhile does nothing. Seems curious, doesn't it?'

'Jolly curious,' said Cartwright frowning. 'You mean he had plenty of time to give the alarm when he found that the 'phone had been tampered with?'

'Yes,' answered his employer. 'He must have guessed who was responsible, and it seems inconceivable to suppose he just sat there and waited for me to come along, fully aware that the 'Phantom Slayer' had discovered that he knew something and would either make good his escape or do something to stop him talking.'

'It does sound absurd,' agreed Cartwright.

'It's preposterous,' replied Blackmore, and a short silence fell between them which was broken at length by the secretary.

'I say,' he said suddenly, 'do you think the 'Phantom Slayer' could have mistaken the flat — got into Mellish's thinking it was Falkner's, I mean. It would have been quite easy in the dark to have misjudged the window, they're both alike and close together.'

'I did not think of that,' said John nodding, 'but when you come to analyse it it's not tenable. It couldn't have been a mistake, you forget the brace and bit. That was brought specially for the purpose, to bore the hole through the wall, therefore the whole crime must have been premeditated and carefully thought out'

Cartwright nodded.

'The thing that strikes me as most peculiar,' Blackmore continued, 'is the fact that the murderer having killed his victim should have remained in Mellish's flat for as long as he did. We were there for a considerable time before he made his getaway, and instead of rushing out from the front door, it would have been far easier, and much less risky, if he had escaped the same way as he came — by the window.'

'It beats me,' declared Harry with a gesture of despair. 'I can't make head or tail of it.'

'Let us hope,' said his employer, 'that the watch will prove to be a clue. I'm under the impression that once we've established the identity of the 'Slayer' everything else will automatically come clear.'

He paused, a belated taxi was speeding towards them and John hailed it, settling back on the cushions with a sigh of relief. He remained silent during the journey to Mecklinburg Square, gazing unseeingly at the rain-blurred window, while his secretary occupied his mind with the strange events of the evening, without, however, coming to any satisfactory conclusion. The cab stopping opposite the familiar house roused Blackmore from his reverie, and descending wearily, for he felt dead tired, he paid the driver, and walking up the steps to the front door inserted his key in the lock. He was in the act of turning it when something, a sixth sense, seemed to breathe a warning in his ear. He stopped, with the key half turned, and it was as well that he did, for at the same instant his eyes became attracted to the letter box.

A curious irregular, green stain darkened the usually highly polished brass. With a sharp intake of his breath Blackmore bent down and pushed open the letter flap.

'Run,' he shouted to Cartwright, and with a quick jerk of his wrist twisted the key and flung the door wide open.

Leaping back down the steps he joined his astonished secretary on the edge of the pavement. From the open doorway poured a cloud of greenish, yellow vapour. Blackmore's face set grimly as a whiff of it was borne to his nostrils. The hall was full of poison gas and he knew from the odour that it had been put there by the 'Phantom Slayer.'

5

The Disappearance of Charles Alden

Although it had been in the small hours of the morning before he had gone to bed, John Blackmore was up to time, and eight o'clock found him seated at the breakfast table engaged in helping himself to his favourite grilled kidneys his cook had provided. He looked pale and haggard, and there were dark blue circles round his eyes, and lines about his mouth that spoke eloquently of the strain through which he had lived during the past week, for Blackmore, when he was engaged upon a case was indefatigable. He would scarcely eat or sleep until he had brought the particular problem in hand to a successful conclusion, and over the affair of the 'Phantom Slayer' he had expended more energy than usual.

For weeks he had worked to bring the unknown murderer to justice, using every resource at his command, but without result.

The murder of Falkner had been the culmination in a long series of crimes, and Blackmore had to admit that he was baffled. The attempt on his own life on the previous night, or rather morning, troubled him little. It had been some hours before the gas had sufficiently dispersed to enable his secretary and himself to enter the house, and even now the peculiar smell still hung about the hall and staircase. The method by which the gas had been introduced was obvious, and John concluded from his subsequent examination that it had been brought in a cylinder, the nozzle of which had been inserted through the letter box and the gas released. The whole operation would scarcely have taken five minutes, and at that hour the man who had carried out the plan would have run very little risk — except the chance of being challenged by a patrolling police-man, and in all probability he had timed his visit so as to be in between the rounds. The servants slept in the upper part of the building and so had been safe, for the gas was heavier than air and there was not sufficient to fill more than the hall. Had anything, however, disturbed any of them and brought them down nothing could have saved their lives.

Blackmore pushed aside his scarcely tasted breakfast, poured himself out a second cup of coffee and rising to his feet walked over to the mantelpiece and helped himself to a cigarette from the box that was there. When it was alight he picked up a copy of the *Megaphone* and glanced at George Mellish's account of the murder at Evesham Mansions. The reporter had let himself go, and flaring headlines splashed over three columns. As a piece of journalese it was excellent stuff, and John had just finished reading the last words when a maid tapped at the door and ushered in Inspector Kenton.

The Scotland Yard man bustled into the room in a great state of excitement, banged his bowler hat on the table, making the crockery dance. Blackmore laid down the paper and shook hands.

'You're an early caller, Kenton,' he remarked with a slight smile.

The inspector nodded his bristly head.

'Couldn't wait for you to come round, John,' he jerked, warming his fat, stubby hands at the fire, for a sharp frost had succeeded the rain of the previous night. 'What's this latest exploit of the 'Phantom Slayer's,' eh? I've just had a report through from Divisional Inspector Heel, but it doesn't say much, only the bare facts. Understand you were on the spot, and thought I'd drop in and get all details from you before going along.'

'I was very much on the spot,' said John, 'but I'm afraid I can tell you little more than Heel. Have some coffee.'

He poured out a cup, the inspector took it, gulped down the steaming fluid gratefully. He set the empty cup down and perched himself on the arm of a chair while Blackmore told him as briefly as possible all he knew of the murder of Falkner. Kenton listened attentively, and when the other had finished he ran his fingers through his hair.

'Pity that fellow got away,' he grunted.

'Would have put an end to all our troubles if he hadn't.'

'It's a thousand pities,' agreed Blackmore, 'but it couldn't be helped, and we may be able to trace him through the watch.'

Kenton pursed his rather thick lips.

'You can't be certain that it belonged to him,' he objected, 'and even if it did it's a hundred to one that the jewellers will remember to whom it was sold.'

'My dear fellow, don't be pessimistic,' said Blackmore. 'It's a chance, anyhow, and well worth following up. Even if it comes to nothing it can do no harm.'

'This 'Phantom Slayer' business is getting on my nerves,' grunted the inspector. 'There'll be a row at Headquarters over this last affair. The Assistant Commissioner's like a bear with a sore head lately, and this isn't going to make him any better tempered.'

Blackmore nodded sympathetically.

'I know, it's unpleasant for you,' he said. 'But we can only hope that something will happen soon that will enable us to get on the right track. He can't go on for ever without making a mistake, it isn't humanly possible. Up to now he's had abnormal luck, and sooner or later it's bound to fail him.'

'Well, I'd rather it was sooner than later,' growled Kenton. 'I wonder what it was that Falkner found out.'

'I think it was the 'Phantom Slayer's' identity,' replied John, 'and that's the reason why he was killed.'

'I'd like to know how he managed it,' snorted the inspector. 'Must have been a jolly sight cleverer than we are.' He picked up his hat and crammed it savagely on his bullet head. 'Well, I'll be getting along,' he said. 'Will you let me know at once if you learn anything further?'

'Of course,' answered Blackmore. 'If you'll wait a moment I'll come part of the way with you.'

Without waiting for a reply he went upstairs into his bedroom and quickly exchanged the smoking jacket he was wearing for a tweed one, and before coming back to Kenton glanced into Cartwright's room. Tired out with his night's exertion, the secretary was still sleeping peacefully. Blackmore closed the door softly without disturbing him and hurried down the stairs. He was pulling on his overcoat when Kenton sniffed the air several times.

'Peculiar smell,' he remarked. 'You been doing some experiments in chemistry or something?'

Blackmore smiled grimly as he opened the front door.

'No,' he replied. 'The experiment was carried out by the 'Phantom Slayer,' but luckily it didn't come off.'

'What do you mean?' asked the inspector in astonishment.

Blackmore told him of the episode of the poison gas while they walked along, and Kenton's rather prominent eyes almost started from his head.

'Good God!' he ejaculated. 'What a ghastly thing. Why, he might have killed the whole household.'

Blackmore nodded.

'I doubt very much if he would care if he had,' he replied. 'We've ample proof that the 'Phantom Slayer' regards human life — like that — ' he snapped his fingers.

'And he'd murder his way out of any difficulty.'

'I wonder who he can be, John,' said the inspector, rubbing at his moustache. 'I've gone through the whole list of known criminals and I can't hit on any likely person.'

'You won't,' answered Blackmore decidedly. 'I'm convinced that the 'Phantom Slayer' is altogether a new figure in the annals of crime. His method is quite apart from anything we have ever known before, and you are perfectly well aware that every big criminal — I'm not talking about the petty crooks — has his own particular way of working. His crimes are stamped with his personality in most cases as clearly as if he had left his signature behind.'

'Yes, that's true,' agreed Kenton. 'I'm inclined to take your view, that we are up against some one entirely new.'

'There's another reason and a good one why I think that,' Blackmore went on. 'You know I've spent a considerable time lately frequenting all sorts of well-known criminal haunts, disguised, in the hopes

71

of lighting on a chance clue that would lead me to the 'Slayer.''

Kenton nodded quickly.

'Well, the crooks are just as keen to find out who he is as we are, and if they knew his life wouldn't be worth a moment's purchase. They're scared because they are not sure who is going to be the next victim. Now, if the 'Phantom Slayer' wasn't a new man they'd have spotted him before now.'

'I think you're right,' said the inspector, 'but it makes it all the more difficult to catch him.'

'We'll catch him — in time,' replied Blackmore. 'It's just a question of patience.'

They parted company at Holborn, Kenton going on to Evesham Mansions, and Blackmore boarding a bus to take him citywards. He got off at Cannon Street Station and walked up in search of Beal and Son. He found the shop about halfway up on the left-hand side, and entering sent in his card to the manager. After a short wait he was ushered into a comfortably furnished office and a stout, bald-headed man seated behind a big desk littered with papers, rose and held out his hand.

'Good morning, Mr. Blackmore,' he said courteously. 'Won't you sit down?'

He pushed forward a chair, and when John was seated, 'Now, what can I have the pleasure of doing for you?'

Blackmore produced the wrist watch from his pocket and laid it on the desk.

'This, I believe, was originally manufactured by your firm,' he said, 'and I should like to know if you can tell me to whom it was sold.'

The manager picked it up and looked at it.

'Yes, it was made by us,' he replied. 'There should be very little difficulty in giving you the information you require.' He opened the back and glanced at the number, then leaning forward he pressed a bell in the desk. 'Ask Mr. Lurgan if he can see me for a minute,' he said to the clerk who answered the summons. 'That's our sales manager,' he explained to John when the man had departed on his errand. 'He has control of our stock and will be able to tell you all you want to know.'

Blackmore thanked him.

'I suppose it's no use asking you what is at the back of this enquiry?' the manager continued, holding out a case of cigarettes.

Blackmore took one and lit it.

'I don't see why not,' he answered with a smile, slowly blowing out a cloud of smoke, and proceeded briefly to tell his interested listener how the watch had come into his possession. He had barely concluded when the door opened and a tall, thin man with iron grey hair and a slight stoop entered. This turned out to be Mr. Lurgan and the manager introduced them. Blackmore repeated his enquiry concerning the watch, and the sales manager peered at it short-sightedly and inclined his head.

'If you will come with me,' he said, 'I'll ascertain the name of the firm this was supplied to.'

Accompanied by the manager, whose interest had been keenly aroused, Blackmore followed Lurgan down a short corridor into a large room in which several clerks were working. The sales manager walked over to a shelf of ledgers at the far end, gazed at them for a second, selected one and carried it over to a desk nearby. He opened the thick book and rapidly turned the pages. About halfway through he stopped, and ran his finger down a list of numbers.

'Here you are,' he said, '10237 — ten watches numbered from 10230 to 10240, were sold to Churlambs, Oxford Street, six months ago.'

Blackmore verified the entry and wrote down the name in his pocketbook.

'Thanks very much,' he said. 'I'm sorry to have given you this trouble.'

'No trouble at all,' replied the sales manager closing the ledger with a snap and replacing it on the shelf. He shook hands and Blackmore took his leave.

The bald-headed manager accompanied him down to the entrance.

'I hope you're successful at Churlambs',' he remarked. 'You should be. It's only a small shop, and I don't think they do a very flourishing business, so it's all the more likely that they will be able to remember who purchased that watch.'

'If they don't, I shall have had all my trouble for nothing,' said Blackmore.

Saying goodbye to the manager he hailed a taxi, and instructing the driver to take him to Oxford Circus was soon being driven westwards. So far his progress had been satisfactory, it now remained to see what there was to be learned from Churlambs. If they could remember to whom they had sold the watch his chase of the 'Phantom Slayer' was nearing its conclusion. Always supposing that the watch had belonged to the unknown murderer. There was an element of doubt regarding this, but John was fairly certain that it had not been there when he and Cartwright had arrived at Evesham Mansions. It was in a fairly conspicuous position when his secretary had found it, and John felt sure he would have noticed it had it been there before. Unless, therefore, some of the other tenants had dropped it either coming or going in the meanwhile, it was only reasonable to suppose that it had fallen from the wrist of the unknown man while he was making his escape from Mellish's flat, and everything seemed to point to the fact that this individual was the 'Phantom Slayer' himself.

He descended from the taxi at Oxford Circus, dismissed it and walked up towards Marble Arch. Churlambs proved to be a small jeweller's sandwiched in between two large department stores on the right, and pushing open the glass panel door Blackmore entered. An elderly man with nearly white hair and wearing a pair of gold pince-nez perched on the extreme tip of his rather large nose, looked up from his examination of a tray of rings as he did so. He listened while John stated his business and then pursed his thin lips dubiously.

'I don't know whether I can help you,' he said in a high, reedy voice. 'We have such a number of chance customers it would be impossible to remember them all. Let me see the watch.'

Blackmore unwrapped it and handed it to the jeweller.

'H'm,' said the elderly man, examining

it carefully. 'This is one of the ten we had from Beal, they sold very well. In fact I've just ordered some more. I'm afraid I can't tell you who had this one unless — ' He paused. 'I believe one of the watches was bought by a lady as a present for her husband and we sent it to her flat, I'll look up the books and make sure.'

He went behind the glass partition, and John waited impatiently. Was the clue going to end in a blind alley after all? After some little time the old jeweller reappeared carrying an open book in his hand.

'You're lucky,' he said with a wintry smile. 'This is the watch I was speaking about. The one we sent to the lady.'

'What was the name and address?' asked John, his pulses beating a trifle quicker.

The jeweller consulted the book.

'Mrs. Alden,' he said. 'Twenty-eight Harley Terrace, Edward Road, Marble Arch.'

Blackmore thanked him and left the shop feeling elated, in search of Harley Terrace. His luck had held good and in a little while he would know for certain whether the watch had any connection with the 'Phantom Slayer' or whether he had, after all, been following up a false clue.

Harley Terrace was a rather narrow street leading off the Edgware Road about two hundred yards from Marble Arch, and number twenty-eight turned out to be a house that had evidently been turned into flats, for alongside the main door was a row of shining bell pushes, against each one of which was a name engraved on a small brass plate. Blackmore quickly found the name he was seeking, C. Alden, and pressing the corresponding button, waited. There was a long pause and he was in the act of raising his hand to ring again when he heard the sound of swift footsteps, and the door opened. A girl stood on the threshold, she was tall and slim, with oval features and brown-gold hair. Her large eyes surveyed him with surprise, and, he thought, a trace of apprehension.

'Mrs. Alden?' he enquired, raising his hat.

She nodded her head.

'I am Mrs. Alden. What do you want?'

Blackmore noticed that her face was deathly pale and that her eyes were heavy lidded, and showed signs of recent tears.

'I should like to have a word or two with you, if I may,' he said.

She looked at him steadily for a moment or two before replying.

'What — what was it you wanted to see me about?' Her voice was low, almost inaudible, and she made no attempt to ask him in.

John took the little wristlet watch from his pocket.

'I wanted to see you about this — ' he began, holding it in his open palm, but he got no further. The girl gave a smothered cry and her already pale face went a ghastly white. She swayed and clutched at the door for support with trembling hands.

'What's the matter?' exclaimed Blackmore quickly, 'are you ill?'

'Where did you get that?' she asked in a husky whisper, her wide eyes fixed on the watch in his hand. 'Tell me, where did you get it?'

'Do you recognise it?' asked John.

She seemed to find a difficulty in speaking, for it was some time before she replied.

'Yes, it — it belongs to my husband. How did you come by it. Has there been an accident?'

The last words were practically incoherent, choked by a sob that rose in her throat. A glimmer of the reason for her agitation suddenly found its way into Blackmore's brain.

'Why should you think there has been an accident?' he asked gently.

She raised her eyes.

'Because my husband has disappeared,' she answered faintly.

6

The Warning Message

John Blackmore had anticipated her reply and waiting for a moment until she had mastered her emotions he leaned forward.

'Don't you think it would be better if we went up to your flat?' he suggested, 'instead of talking here. You can then tell me all about it. My name is Blackmore. Here is my card.'

She looked at the little strip of pasteboard in amazement.

'A detective,' she breathed, and then, 'please come in. I should have asked you before, but I've been so worried, terribly worried, and the sight of my — my husband's watch gave me a dreadful shock.'

She closed the door behind him and he followed her up the stairs. She moved as though uncertain of her limbs, and more than once during the short climb she paused and rested, her hand on the banister rail for support. Her flat was on the third floor, and she ushered him into a tastefully furnished sitting room. His keen eyes noted that the table was laid for a meal, with places set for two people, and that it had evidently been untouched. The girl, she could scarcely have been more than twenty-two, sank down into a low chair and motioned for him to take the one opposite her.

'Now, Mrs. Alden,' he said when she was seated, 'I think the first thing you can do is to tell me exactly what has happened. You say your husband has disappeared.'

'Yes,' she answered, twisting her fingers nervously in her lap. 'He went out about six o'clock last night and I haven't seen him since.'

'Has he ever stayed away like this before?' asked John.

She shook her head.

'No, never — that's why I'm so frightened. I'm sure something terrible has happened to him.' She leaned forward suddenly. 'You must know where he is or you wouldn't have his watch.'

'I'm afraid I don't know,' answered Blackmore. 'I found the watch.'

'You found it, where?' she breathed quickly. He hesitated for a second. 'You're trying to keep something back from me,' she said, noting his hesitation. 'You do know what has happened to Charlie and you won't tell me.'

'Believe me, Mrs. Alden,' said John earnestly, 'I know no more than you. I'm speaking the actual truth when I say that I found this watch.'

She looked at him piteously, her eyes bright with unshed tears.

'Tell me where you found it?' she faltered.

He thought rapidly, her emotion on the face of it seemed genuine enough, and as far as he could see it would do little harm to inform her of the place where the watch had been found. If she was playing a part she in all probability knew already, and if she was not — and he could scarcely bring himself to think she was — then she might be able to supply him with some vital information. He decided at any rate to chance it.

'I found it, or rather my secretary found it,' he said, 'at the entrance to a block of flats in Maida Vale, Evesham Mansions.'

He watched her keenly as he spoke to see what effect his words had. She stared at him, her eyes wide with surprise.

'Evesham Mansions?' she repeated. 'But what could Charlie have been doing there?'

Apparently she had heard nothing of the murder, and John concluded that she hadn't seen the papers that morning. There was no purpose to be gained by enlightening her so he continued.

'Yes. Had your husband any friends or relations living in that neighbourhood?'

She shook her head.

'I never heard him mention any,' she replied.

'Didn't he say where he was going when he went out?' asked John.

'No,' answered the girl. 'He said he might be late, but that's all.'

'And you've no idea where he was going or what he went for?'

She shook her head again.

'I feel certain that something terrible has happened to him,' she said brokenly. 'Otherwise he would never have stopped away like this without letting me know — sending me some message.'

Blackmore was silent for a moment. If his suspicions were correct and Charles Alden was the man who had left Mellish's flat so hurriedly on the previous night, he had every reason for stopping away without revealing his whereabouts.

'I've been up all night,' she went on, holding back her tears by a great effort, 'expecting him to come in every moment. What do you think can have happened to him?'

'There may be quite a simple explanation, Mrs. Alden,' said Blackmore, though his voice lacked conviction. 'Your husband may have been detained, and been unable to let you know.'

'But the watch?' she turned her pale face towards him. 'How do you account for that?'

'It might easily have dropped from his wrist without his being aware of the fact,'

John replied. 'Have you noticed anything in his behaviour lately that might supply a reason for this sudden disappearance?'

'He has seemed rather worried during this last week,' she answered.

'Worried? How?'

'Abstracted and moody, as though something were weighing on his mind,' said the girl. 'I tried several times to get him to tell me what it was, but he always evaded an answer.'

'Can it have been financial trouble?' asked the detective.

'Oh, no,' she answered at once. 'Charlie was quite well off.'

'What was his business?' he enquired. 'Perhaps something in connection with that has kept him.'

'He hadn't any,' she answered. 'He possessed a private income.'

'H'm!'

Blackmore rubbed his chin reflectively. It seemed obvious to him that there was only one reason for Charles Alden's absence, and that was fear — fear that he would be implicated in the murder of Falkner, and if that were the case then it appeared equally obvious that he was the 'Phantom Slayer.'

'Have you informed the police of your husband's disappearance?' he asked.

'No, I haven't told anyone. I've been hoping every moment that he'd come back.' Her voice broke and the tears overflowed, in spite of her efforts to check them, and ran slowly down her cheeks.

'Come, come, Mrs. Alden,' said John kindly. 'You mustn't upset yourself.' He paused while she made an effort to master her emotions and then went on: 'I think it would be as well if his description was circulated. Have you a recent photograph?'

'Yes, Charlie had one taken a month ago.'

Brushing aside her tears she rose to her feet, crossed to a little writing desk by the side of the window, and unlocking it she searched in the interior, and presently returned with a photograph which she handed to him.

It was that of a man about thirty-five, dark, with hair brushed straight back from his rather high forehead. His thin-lipped mouth was shadowed by a small, military moustache. His eyes were large but rather too near the bridge of the aquiline nose to be wholly pleasant. Altogether, thought John, it was the face of a man whom he would not have trusted a yard. At first glance he was not impressed with Mr. Charles Alden.

'May I keep this?' he asked.

The girl nodded and he slipped it into his breast pocket. He put a few more questions but could gather nothing further that was likely to help, and after a short while, with a promise that he would let her know if he heard any news of the missing man, he took his departure.

His first action on leaving the house was to enter a public telephone box, which he had previously noted at the end of the road, and put a call through to Mecklinburg Square. It was Cartwright who answered, and to his secretary John briefly related the morning's adventures, concluding by arranging with Harry to meet him at the corner of Harley Terrace immediately. Leaving the box, he strolled into Edgware Road and halting beside a bus stop lighted a cigarette and awaited his secretary's arrival. His object in sending for him was one of precaution; in his own mind he was convinced that Mrs. Alden was genuinely worried concerning the whereabouts of her husband, but at the same time there was always the possibility that he was mistaken, and that her apparent emotion was merely the outcome of a piece of consummate acting. In this case, if she knew the whereabouts of Alden there was a distinct possibility that she would try and communicate with him in some way in order to inform him of Blackmore's visit, and therefore it was worthwhile setting Cartwright to watch the house and keep an eye on her movements. And even if, as Blackmore believed, she didn't know there was the chance that Charles Alden might send some word to his wife to relieve the anxiety that he must know she was feeling. In either event a close surveillance of the house in Harley Terrace was necessary.

He was fairly certain that Charles Alden and the mysterious individual known as the 'Phantom Slayer' were one and the same, and if this was so motive for his disappearance was obvious. He had discovered the loss of the watch, and guessing where he had dropped it had been afraid that it would be traced. There was no doubt that the watch was Alden's property, and if the man was not connected with the tragedy at Evesham Mansions there wasn't any object in his keeping away.

Blackmore reviewed the whole case while he waited, going over it again and again, and the more he thought about it the surer he became that Charles Alden was the unknown murderer. He was still turning the matter over in his mind when a taxi drew up at the corner of Harley Terrace and he saw Cartwright jump cheerily out. He crossed the road, and when the secretary dismissed the cab, took him by the arm and led him up the street for a short distance.

'I want you to keep an eye on number twenty-eight,' he said, 'and note everybody who goes in or comes out. If Mrs. Alden should leave the house follow her.'

He gave a brief but vivid description of the girl. 'I'll send Brand to relieve you at six o'clock; if anything important happens before then you can phone me at home.'

Cartwright nodded, his eyes sparkling, for there was nothing he liked more than the prospect of adventure.

'Right you are,' he replied. 'Anything else?'

'Yes.' Blackmore took the photograph from his pocket and showed it to his secretary. 'Keep a good look out for anyone remotely resembling this.'

Harry looked at it, noting every detail of the man's features.

'Is that Alden?' he asked.

'That's Alden,' answered Blackmore. 'And unless I'm greatly mistaken that's also the man who broke into Mellish's flat and killed Falkner.'

'The 'Phantom Slayer'?' said the secretary.

'Yes,' replied John. 'I think we've discovered his identity at last. I'm taking this photograph along to the Yard to have it circulated, with the description of the man, and before many days are passed we ought to have the 'Phantom Slayer' safely under lock and key.'

He chatted for a few seconds longer, and then, leaving Cartwright at his post of vigil, he hailed a taxi and was driven to Scotland Yard.

His interview with Inspector Kenton, who had returned from Maida Vale, was short, but it left that worthy man in a state bordering on elation, and two hours after John had left the grim building on the Embankment the photograph of Charles Alden, together with a full description, was locked in the forme of every newspaper in the country.

Making his way home, Blackmore ate a light lunch and afterwards settled down to deal with his neglected correspondence of the morning. There was nothing of much importance, and an hour's work cleared off the few letters that required immediate replies. Having got through these, Blackmore rose from his desk with a sigh of relief, and lighting a cigarette, sank down in his favourite armchair and allowed his mind to turn once more to the case on which he was engaged. But he was destined not to remain undisturbed for long. Scarcely had he got comfortable when the arrival of George Mellish was announced.

The reporter entered the room with a cheery smile, though his usually florid face was pale and wan.

'Thought I'd just drop in and see if you had any fresh news,' he greeted. 'Hope I'm not bothering you?'

'Not at all, my dear fellow, sit down.' He motioned to a chair. 'You look pretty well fagged out.'

'I haven't had a chance to get much sleep,' said Mellish, dropping into the chair and stretching out his legs to the fire. 'Spent most of the night at the *Megaphone* office.'

Blackmore blew out a cloud of smoke, and watched it disperse.

'I read your account of the affair,' he remarked.

'What did you think of it?'

'Excellent.' A faint smile curved Blackmore's lips. 'Particularly the vivid description of the attack on yourself and the terrible danger you were in.''

The reporter grinned.

'They like that sort of stuff,' he said with a chuckle. 'You can't make it too thick. Have you come across any new developments?'

John nodded.

'Several,' he replied, 'but most of them are not for publication at present.'

Mellish looked interested.

'I promise you I won't put pen to paper until you give me the word,' he said. 'But I'd like to hear anything you've discovered to satisfy my own curiosity. I've got a sort of personal interest in this business.' He fingered his head tenderly.

'Well, if you're prepared to keep it to yourself and not splash it in that infernal paper of yours,' said Blackmore, 'I'll tell you. But I warn you, if I see so much as a word in print I'll — I'll have you arrested for interfering with the course of justice.'

'All right, go ahead, I'll be as dumb as an oyster,' answered Mellish, and Blackmore proceeded to recount all that had happened since the reporter had left Evesham Mansions on the previous night.

At the end of his narrative Mellish gave

vent to a low whistle.

'By Jove! You haven't wasted much time,' he exclaimed. 'There doesn't seem much doubt that this fellow Alden is the 'Phantom Slayer'.'

'I don't see how there can be,' said John thoughtfully. 'Unless there were two people in your flat last night, and that's scarcely probable.'

'What beats me,' said the reporter, 'is Falkner's object in having the flat at Evesham Mansions at all. I've puzzled my brains to think out a sensible explanation and I can't.'

Blackmore drew at his cigarette for several seconds in silence before replying.

'It's a point that has also caused me a considerable amount of conjecture,' he murmured at length, staring at the glowing coals. 'As a matter of fact I was waiting to talk to you about it, if you hadn't come in I was going to ring you up.'

Mellish looked at him in astonishment.

'How could I help you?' he asked.

'You've been living at Evesham Mansions for some time, haven't you?' asked Blackmore.

'Yes, nearly three years,' answered the reporter. 'Why?'

'Only that you must be pretty well acquainted with the people who occupy the other flats in the building,' said John. 'For instance, who are your immediate neighbours above and below?'

'There's Colonel Wells, and Mr. and Mrs. Colville on the ground floor,' said Mellish. 'A fellow called Stillman and an elderly maiden lady have the two flats just under mine.' He checked them off on his fingers as he spoke. 'Overhead there's a man named Bryant, he hasn't been there long, about six months, and opposite him two sisters, Denning I think their name is. Then higher up still there's Walkam, he's an actor, then Mr. and Mrs. Roan, that's about all.'

John nodded.

'How many of these people do you know personally?' he enquired.

'None of them,' replied Mellish smiling. 'Of course I'm on speaking terms with nearly all of them — that is, just to say how d'you do, and good night, the usual sort of stuff, but I don't know anything about any of them. What's the idea?'

'I'm merely trying to account for Falkner's presence in the building,' said John. 'He didn't go there to live because he never, as we know, slept there. Obviously he must have had some other reason, and the first one that suggests itself, since he was devoting his time to tracking down the 'Phantom Slayer,' is, that he was there for the purpose of watching someone.'

'Good God!' cried the reporter excitedly. 'I see what you're getting at. You mean that Falkner discovered that the 'Phantom Slayer' was living in the building?'

'Or someone closely connected with him,' answered Blackmore. 'If, as we have reason to believe, Alden is the 'Slayer' it couldn't have been he, because we know that he lives at Harley Terrace. But it appears to be quite possible that he may have had an accomplice who lives at Evesham Mansions, and that it was through this person, whoever it is, that Falkner got on his trail.'

'But you said that the 'Phantom Slayer' always works alone,' protested Mellish.

'So he does, as far as we know,' said Blackmore. 'But he must dispose of the stuff he gets hold of somehow.'

'And you think the fence lives at Evesham Mansions?'

'That's how I work it out,' said John slowly.

'I wonder who it could be?' Mellish wrinkled his forehead in thought. 'It might be Stillman or Bryant, they're fairly new comers.'

'Might be anybody,' said John, 'or I might be entirely wrong. Anyway, I'm having enquiries made about everyone in the building, and the place is under police surveillance, I arranged that with Kenton this morning.'

'I shall have to be careful what I do in future.' Mellish rose to his feet and grinned. 'Well, I think I shall get along and have a sleep, I feel about all in.'

'You certainly look as if you needed it,' said Blackmore, looking critically at the reporter's haggard face.

Mellish shrugged his shoulders.

'You get used to it in time,' he answered. 'I wish I could write up what you've told me, it would make a good story.'

Before Blackmore could reply there came the sharp rat-tat of the postman, and a moment later a maid brought in a little pile of letters. Blackmore rapidly glanced over them. There were several circulars which he tossed aside but one envelope was marked urgent. With a word of apology to Mellish he ripped open the flap and withdrew the contents.

His sudden quick exclamation attracted the reporter's attention.

'What is it?' he cried curiously. For answer, John handed him the single sheet of paper that he had taken from the envelope.

Mellish looked at it, and as he read the typewritten message he drew in his breath swiftly. It began without the preliminary of date or address.

'You escaped death last night by luck. You will not do so always. Be warned and leave me alone. The next time I shall not fail.'

There was no signature, but neither of them was in doubt as to whom the letter emanated from.

'The 'Phantom Slayer,'' breathed Mellish softly.

Blackmore nodded, and the expression on his face was grim and stern.

'That's a reminder of last night's little gas episode,' he remarked. 'Our friend has learned of my enquiries and is getting nervous.' He picked up the envelope, carried it over to the window and scrutinised the post mark. 'Posted this morning. W.1. district,' he muttered. 'That doesn't help us much.' He laid the envelope down and taking up the letter closely examined it, first with the naked eye and through a powerful pocket lens. 'He's used the same typewriter as all the other communications were written on,' he said after a while. 'A Remington — there's no mistaking that chipped P or the E slightly out of alignment.'

He pointed out the errors as he spoke to Mellish who had crossed over to his side.

'He's certainly got a nerve,' said the

reporter. 'What are you going to do about this?'

Blackmore tossed the letter on to his desk and shrugged his shoulders.

'Nothing,' he replied. 'I've had too many such warnings during my time to let it worry me.'

'But you ought to take precautions,' said Mellish. 'I'm certain it's no idle threat, just theatrical bluff. He means business, and he's already made one attempt.'

'I know,' said John, 'and of course I shall keep a sharp lookout. If, as we think, this man Alden is the 'Phantom Slayer' he'll have all his work cut out at the moment trying to avoid capture, without turning his attention to me.'

Mellish raised his eyebrows.

'That letter was written this morning,' he said, 'and he must have known at the time he posted it, that in all probability you had succeeded in tracing the watch. If, as you imagine, he is lying low, what was the object in sending it at all?'

'I should say,' answered John, thoughtfully, 'that his main object was to try and shake my nerve. He himself is in a panic, and he wants to try and create the same state of affairs in the enemy's camp. There's nothing like getting your opponent rattled. It's the surest way of stopping him thinking clearly, and that is what our friend is trying to do with me.'

'You're probably right,' agreed the reporter, 'but at the same time he's undoubtedly dangerous and I should certainly be on my guard if I were you.' He glanced at the clock. 'Well, I must be off, or I shan't have any time for a rest. I've got to be at the office at seven. Let me know if you discover anything about the people at Evesham Mansions, and give me the wire just as soon as I can print the story.'

'I'll come part of the way with you,' said John. 'I've got some letters I want to post.'

Mellish waited while he gathered up the little pile of correspondence and pulled on his overcoat, and then together they made their way down the stairs and out into the street.

Dusk was falling and there was a tang of frost in the air. The square was almost devoid of traffic, and as they walked along John and Mellish continued their conversation regarding the latest development in the case. They were still discussing it when John reached the pillar box that had been his objective. Breaking off in the middle of a remark to the reporter he stopped, took his letters from his pocket and slipped them into the slit provided for the purpose. He was in the act of turning to finish his sentence when a sharp staccato explosion of a motorcycle's exhaust attracted his attention. He looked back up the street. The machine was travelling towards them at a fair speed, the driver crouched low over the handlebars.

'That fellow will get pulled up soon,' said Mellish, as the cyclist drew level with them. 'There must be something wrong with the silencer — ' He broke off with a sharp cry of pain, reeled, and clapped his hand to his arm.

'What's the matter?' asked Blackmore quickly. The next moment he knew, for another bullet whistled past his ear and there was a crash of glass as a window behind them shattered into fragments.

The 'Phantom Slayer' had made his second attempt.

7

The Death Shot

It was late on the following morning, and Blackmore paced up and down his study with long, nervous strides, a cigarette between his lips, his hands clasped behind his back, oblivious of everything but the problem that was exercising his mind. Every now and again he stopped mechanically by the window and gazed out into the quiet square.

He was feeling irritable, and his brain persisted in thinking in circles. There was not the slightest doubt that the attempt on his life on the previous afternoon had been a carefully planned attack by the 'Phantom Slayer.' He was convinced that the two shots had been fired by the motorcyclist as he passed, under cover of the noise made by the exhaust, but before he had time to recover from the first shock of surprise the motorcycle had disappeared. And all subsequent enquiries had failed to place it.

Mellish had received a nasty wound in the fleshy part of his arm, but luckily the bullet had missed the muscle, and beyond causing the reporter a certain amount of pain and inconvenience, it had done little serious damage. After having it dressed at a nearby chemist's he had hurried off to write up an account of the incident for the *Megaphone*, rather jubilant than otherwise, that such an excellent piece of copy had been delivered into his hands.

John had explained what had occurred to the constable who came running up at the sound of the breaking glass, and leaving him to deal with the irate owner whose house had been thus damaged, he had returned to his own home to await the arrival of Cartwright, from his vigil outside the flat at Harley Terrace. Although he had expected nothing in particular to accrue, Blackmore couldn't help feeling vaguely disappointed at his secretary's report. No one had attempted to call at the house who in any way could have been remotely associated with

Alden, and although the girl herself had gone out during the latter part of the afternoon it had only been in order to make a few purchases at the shop round the corner.

The report from Burk, the man who had taken Cartwright's place, was just as unsatisfactory when he 'phoned through late the same night, and the secretary had nothing further to relate when he returned that morning, tired out and weary from his night's unprofitable occupation.

Blackmore felt that he was up against a blank wall, and he could do nothing but wait with as much patience as possible in the hope that the police would receive some news of the missing Alden. But nothing had come through as yet, although the man's description had appeared in both the evening and morning editions of the papers.

To a man of John Blackmore's energetic nature the enforced inactivity was galling in the extreme, and the feeling of absolute impotence played on his nerves until they were reduced to shreds, and in consequence his temper was not of the sweetest. The months of ceaseless toil he had put in trying to run the 'Phantom Slayer' to earth were beginning to tell, even on his constitution, and the strain was becoming unbearable.

Throughout the entire morning he paced up and down the room, pausing only to light a fresh cigarette or to answer the summons of the telephone, hoping each time the bell rang that it was Kenton ringing up with some information regarding the missing man. Lunch time came and with the arrival of the meal Cartwright entered the dining room, refreshed from his long morning's sleep. He tried his utmost to get his employer to enter into a conversation, but John merely answered with brief monosyllables, and refusing all food, sat in thoughtful silence.

Cartwright knew by experience that it was useless to attempt to do anything when his employer was in this mood, and eventually relapsed into silence.

He did full justice to the substantial luncheon, however, and shortly afterwards took his departure to return to

Harley Terrace, and relieve Burk upon number twenty-eight.

For an hour after his departure Blackmore roamed about the study like a caged bear, and then, with a shrug of his shoulders he threw away his half smoked cigarette, struggled into his overcoat and left the house.

He had decided that a brisk walk would in all probability do much to disperse his depression, and the exercise prove beneficial to his overstrained nerves.

With a supreme effort of will he forgot the whole case. Making his way to Oxford Street he turned up towards Marble Arch and presently found himself in the Park. It was a perfect winter's afternoon, the air clean and crisp and it acted like a tonic on Blackmore as he strode with long swinging strides across the velvety grass. He made a complete circuit of the Park and the red globe of the sun was sinking into a bank of purple mist before he returned to his starting point, and set off for home.

The walk had acted like a sedative, by the time John reached Mecklinburg

Square he was almost his calm normal self. As he entered his study the telephone bell rang, and crossing to the instrument he lifted the receiver. The voice of Detective Inspector Kenton came over the wire.

'Hello. Is that you, Blackmore?' it said.

John replied in the affirmative.

'I believe we've found Alden,' continued the inspector. 'Can you come along to the Yard?'

'I'll be with you in ten minutes,' answered John, and hanging up the black cylinder, he hurried once more into the street.

An empty taxi was passing, and hailing it he gave the directions to the driver and the next second was running swiftly along in the direction of Whitehall. In two minutes over the time he had stipulated he was in Kenton's office, shaking hands with the inspector.

'We've just had a message from the Royal Free Hospital at Kensington,' said Kenton after a few preliminary remarks. 'It appears that a man was knocked down on the night of Falkner's murder by a taxicab and taken to the hospital suffering from slight concussion. There was nothing on him to identify him, and he has been unconscious ever since. But the house surgeon says that he answers in every way to the description of Alden.'

'Have you seen him?' asked Blackmore.

Kenton shook his head.

'No,' he replied. 'I thought I'd ring you up first, I'm going along now.'

'I'll come with you,' said Blackmore, 'and I think it would be a good idea if we collected Mrs. Alden on the way. We shall need her to identify the man.'

The inspector agreed and reached for his coat.

'If this fellow does turn out to be Alden,' he said, as they made their way down the corridor, 'it rather knocks your theory of his being the 'Phantom Slayer' on the head, doesn't it?'

Blackmore frowned thoughtfully.

'You mean that the reason for his disappearance has been explained satisfactorily?' he answered.

'Yes,' answered Kenton. 'It was the accident that prevented his going home, and not, as we thought, that he was afraid of being traced.'

'But the accident doesn't explain how his watch came to be found at Evesham Mansions,' said Blackmore. 'There's no doubt that he was there at the time, or somewhere near the time that the murder was committed; whatever happened subsequently I should like to hear his explanation. After all, the fact of his being knocked down by a taxi and injured doesn't prove anything. Might be purely a coincidence, I mean it might still have been his intention to disappear, and the accident could easily have occurred while he was putting that intention into practice.'

'Yes, that's true,' agreed Kenton. 'Though you must admit that it would be rather a peculiar coincidence.'

'I could give you instances of much more peculiar coincidences than that,' said Blackmore. 'It's useless wasting time in conjecture until we've seen the man. It may not be Alden at all, but merely someone who bears a chance resemblance to him.'

They had reached the big archway leading into Whitehall while they had been speaking, and Inspector Kenton approached the police car that was waiting, drawn up by the kerb.

'I ordered this while I was waiting for you,' he explained, as he opened the door for John to enter. 'Thought it would be quicker than a taxi. Number twenty-eight, isn't it?'

Blackmore nodded, and the inspector gave the address of Mrs. Alden's flat to the driver, and climbed in beside him.

The car was a powerful one and made short work of the run to Harley Terrace. In a little under fifteen minutes they drew up outside the house occupied by Mrs. Alden and Blackmore and the inspector got out. Cartwright came towards them as they stood on the pavement, his face depicting his astonishment.

'Hello,' he exclaimed. 'I never expected to see you here. What's happened?'

Blackmore told him briefly the object of their visit.

'Can I come with you to the hospital?' he asked when he heard the news. 'There doesn't seem much point on keeping a watch on this place now.'

John shook his head.

'I'm afraid you'll have to stay,' he replied, and the secretary's face fell. 'For all we know, this may prove to be a wild goose chase. Till we're certain that we've found Alden you'd better remain at your post.'

Although he was disappointed Cartwright said nothing. It was dreary work watching the house in Harley Terrace, and he was heartily sick of it. He wouldn't have cared so much if there was a chance of anything happening, but so far the monotony had been unbroken by any exciting incident, and in his heart the secretary believed that it was likely to remain so. However, orders were orders, so with a sigh he turned away as his employer and the inspector ascended the steps to the door of number twenty-eight, and once more took up his position at the corner of the street.

It was Mrs. Alden herself who answered their ring. She looked pale and ill, but started forward eagerly as she recognised Blackmore.

'You have news of Charlie?' she asked quickly, before he had time to speak.

John inclined his head gravely.

'I believe he has been found,' he answered gently. 'A man answering to your husband's description met with an accident the night before last and was taken to the Royal Free Hospital. We want you to come with us and identify him.'

The girl's face blanched and she laid a trembling hand on his arm.

'He isn't — isn't — ' She broke off, her large eyes looking at him questioningly.

'No, no,' he said hurriedly, 'he's alive, and as far as we know, not seriously injured. He has been unconscious, but there is no reason to suppose that he won't completely recover in a week or so.'

'I'll come with you at once,' she said in a low voice. 'Will you wait while I get my hat and coat?'

Without stopping for a reply she turned and hurried up the stairs. In a few moments she reappeared, dressed for the street. They crossed the pavement to the waiting car and getting in once more started off, this time in the direction of Kensington. Blackmore was silent during the short journey for he had much to occupy his thoughts. If the man they were about to see turned out to be Charles Alden after all then he would have to completely change his theories, for since Alden had been unconscious at the hospital for the past two days it was impossible that he could have been the same person who had sent the warning letter, or had attempted his life on the previous afternoon. Therefore, he was not the 'Phantom Slayer.' But then again, what had he been doing at Evesham Mansions on the night of the murder? Could he have been an accomplice of the unknown murderer? It seemed a possible explanation, but Blackmore was disinclined to consider it the true one, for he was practically convinced from his study of the 'Phantom Slayer's' many crimes the man worked alone.

It was a puzzling problem, and the more he analysed it the more puzzling it became. If Alden was not the 'Phantom Slayer' it meant beginning all over again in his search for the elusive criminal, and without the ghost of a clue that was likely to help him.

He checked a weary sigh as he thought of the weeks of ceaseless endeavour that had apparently led to nothing. There was just the possibility that he might learn something from Alden if the man was in a fit state to be questioned, and this, at the moment, was his only hope. He was still pondering about the affair when they arrived at the hospital. Kenton gave his name to the porter, and after a little delay they were conducted into the house surgeon's room.

Doctor Gault was a tall, thin man, on the youngish side, and rose from behind his writing table to meet them.

'It was the nurse who drew my attention to the description in the papers,' he said with a pronounced Scotch accent, 'and of course I immediately got in touch with the Yard. I don't think there can be any doubt that our patient is the man you want.'

'Is he conscious yet?' enquired Black-more.

The doctor nodded.

'He recovered consciousness about two hours ago,' he replied. 'Of course he's still very weak. The wound on his head is rather a nasty one.'

'Is there any danger?' said the girl huskily, trying desperately to keep her voice steady.

'I should say no. That is, of course, unless complications set in, but I don't think that at all likely. It's just a simple case of concussion and very slight at that.'

'Could we see the man?' asked Kenton.

'Yes, I'll take you along at once,' replied the doctor crossing to the door and holding it open for Mrs. Alden to pass through. 'If you'll excuse me I'll lead the way.'

They followed him down a long corridor and up a flight of stone steps, along another passage and turned sharply at right angles and again up a short staircase. He opened a door to the left of the landing and stood aside, motioning for them to enter.

The ward in which they found themselves was a small one, consisting of only three beds, all of them occupied.

'This is what we call an auxiliary ward,' explained Doctor Gault, closing the door. 'We're rather full up just now, and we've had to convert every available inch of spare room to accommodate the overflow of patients. This is the man you want to see.'

He led the way over to the last bed near the window, and the nurse, who had been sitting on a low chair beside it, rose as they approached.

'How is the patient?' asked Gault in a low voice, glancing towards the still form in the bed.

'He's been sleeping, sir,' replied the woman. 'I think he's awake now, he was moving just before you came in.'

The doctor bent over the bed and as he did so the occupant turned slowly. His face was white and drawn, its pallor accentuated by the snowy bandage that covered his head, but there was no mistaking that it was Charles Alden, for the face of the photograph looked up from among the rumpled pillows. With a queer sobbing cry the girl flung herself on her knees beside the bed.

'Charlie, Charlie,' she whispered huskily as she kissed the ashy lips.

The man on the bed stretched out a thin hand.

'Mary,' he said, in a weak, scarcely audible voice. 'Mary.'

Blackmore waited for a moment or two and then stepping forward he laid his hand gently on Mary Alden's shoulder. She turned her tear stained face up to him.

'You recognise this man?' he asked softly, and she nodded.

'Yes, he's my husband,' she managed to murmur in an undertone, though her emotion made the words difficult to catch.

'That's conclusive,' said Kenton, who was standing by John's side.

'Quite,' answered Blackmore. He turned to the doctor. 'Do you think it would be possible for me to put one or two questions to the patient?' he enquired in a low tone.

Doctor Gault looked grave.

'He's far from strong,' he objected. 'Is it very important?'

'Very,' said Blackmore.

'Well, if you can make them as short as possible I don't think there will be much harm,' answered the doctor grudgingly. 'But care must be taken not to overtax his strength.'

Blackmore walked round to the other side of the bed and seated himself on the edge. Charles Alden was holding his wife's hand but he turned his head towards the detective.

'Mr. Alden,' said John in a soothing voice, 'I'm sorry to have to worry you when you're so obviously unfit but it is absolutely essential that I should ask you some questions concerning the night of your accident.'

'Who are you?' said Alden. 'Why do you want to question me?'

'My name is Blackmore,' answered John. 'And I am connected with the police.'

'The police.' The sick man hissed the words as he drew in his breath sharply, and into his wide eyes shot a momentary look of fear.

'I want you to tell me,' continued Blackmore, without appearing to notice his agitation, 'what you were doing in Evesham Mansions?'

Charles Alden's hand closed convulsively on the girl's.

'At Evesham Mansions?' he repeated below his breath.

'Yes.' John leaned forward and looked at him steadily. 'We know you were there because your watch was found in the entrance.' He paused, and as the sick man said nothing he went on: 'Mr. Alden, a murder was committed there that night — a man named Falkner was killed.'

He was watching Alden closely as he spoke and into the man's eyes crept an expression of horrified amazement.

'Murder!' His dry lips could scarcely articulate the sinister word. 'I know nothing about it. Nothing at all.'

'I'm not saying that you do,' said Blackmore slowly. 'I'm only asking you what you were doing at the flat when you lost your watch.'

An appreciable time passed before Alden replied.

'I — I was waiting outside,' he said at length.

'Why?' persisted Blackmore.

There was another silence, this time broken by the girl.

'Why don't you tell the gentleman,' she said gently. 'You've got nothing to conceal, surely. What were you there for Charlie?'

Alden passed the tip of his tongue over his lips.

'I was waiting for a friend,' he said huskily.

Blackmore raised his eyebrows.

'A friend?' he repeated. 'Do you mean someone who occupied a flat in the mansions?'

'No, he didn't live there,' answered Charles Alden. 'He — he went to call on someone.'

'On George Mellish?' Blackmore shot the question suddenly.

'I can't tell you any more,' said Alden feebly.

'Perhaps I can tell you.' John's voice

was hard and metallic. 'Your friend broke into Mellish's flat, attacked him, and after he had rendered him unconscious killed Falkner who occupied the flat next door, by boring a hole through the wall and discharging a gas pistol in his face. Your friend is known as the 'Phantom Slayer'.'

'You're wrong,' said Alden, his voice grew stronger in his excitement. He struggled up on to one elbow. 'I'm not going to tell you who he was, but he was not the 'Phantom Slayer,' he was following the 'Phantom Slayer.' We were both following him — curse him.'

'You were following him?' It was Kenton who spoke. The inspector had been listening intently and now he broke in: 'Do you mean to say you know who the 'Phantom Slayer' is?'

'Yes, I know him,' replied Charles Alden, and his tone was full of hatred, 'and I'll get him one of these days — if I'm still alive.'

'Who is he?' asked Blackmore, and his immobile face betrayed nothing of the excitement he was feeling.

'He's a man called 'Rees',' began

Alden. 'That's his real name, he's known as — ' He broke off as a startled cry came from Doctor Gault.

'Look out all of you!'

John swung round. The doctor was staring at the window, a look of horror in his eyes, and as Blackmore followed his glance he saw the reason. The window was open at the top and through the aperture, between the sash and the frame, there appeared a hand — a black gloved hand, holding an automatic. Blackmore sprung to his feet, but before he could move a step there was a deafening report, and with a choking cry Charles Alden fell back on his pillow, the white bandage round his head slowly crimsoning. Almost before the sound of the shot had died away Blackmore rushed over to the window and flinging it up below a sash, leaned out.

The fire escape ran just below the sill, and straining his eyes in the darkness he made out the shadowy figure of a man hurrying down the iron stairway. Careless of his own danger, John slipped through the window and set off in pursuit, but by the time he reached the ground the figure was nowhere in sight. The escape led down to a small courtyard at the back of the hospital — a place full of packing cases and empty crates. At the far end of the yard he found a narrow door. It was unlocked and opened on to a side turning and it was evidently by this means that the shooter had made his getaway.

Blackmore took the precaution of searching the place, but without any result, and presently he went back up the fire escape and re-entered the ward by way of the window.

'He got clean away,' he said bitterly, in answer to Kenton's enquiry, and crossed over to the bed on which Charles Alden lay.

The girl had fainted and was being attended to by the frightened nurse, but the man who had said that he knew the identity of the 'Phantom Slayer' was dead — killed, with the name of the murderer unspoken on his lips.

8

The Appointment

Four days had elapsed since the killing of Charles Alden in the hospital ward at the moment when he was about to utter a statement that would have supplied the police with the identity of the unknown murderer, and during that period Blackmore had tried everything his keen brain could devise to try and discover some clue that would put him on the track once more of the 'Phantom Slayer.' Alden had said that the man's real name was Rees, and a search of the records at Scotland Yard had revealed some rather interesting information.

Five years previously, a man under the name of Arthur Rees had served eighteen months' imprisonment for robbery with violence, at Pentonville. Apparently it was his first known offence, for there was no list of previous convictions, and the record was unsatisfactorily short. There was a card of fingerprints, but curiously no photograph of the man.

Blackmore had pointed out this discrepancy to Kenton while they had been examining the files, and the inspector had immediately put through an enquiry, but all records could tell them was, that there had been a photograph at one time but that it had either got lost or been destroyed. Considering the thousands in their charge it was not surprising that occasionally one or two should be mislaid, but it was annoying to find that even Fate seemed to play into the hands of the 'Phantom Slayer.'

Blackmore had succeeded in making one fresh discovery, however, and a fairly significant one, though it didn't help him very much at the moment. Mrs. Alden was prostrate with grief, and the tragic death of her husband, but had given John permission to look through his private papers in the hope of finding the name of the man whom Alden had stated had been with him at Evesham Mansions on the night of Falkner's murder. Blackmore had found nothing to enlighten him at the flat, there being little there but receipted bills, and a few old letters, mostly concerning investments that the dead man had made. But at Alden's bank he learned that he had rented a safe for some years, and here he was luckier, for among the various documents and papers it contained he discovered positive proof that Charles Alden's real name had been Leighton.

At first it had conveyed nothing to him, but suddenly he remembered that Leighton had also been the name of one of the 'Phantom Slayer's' early victims. He had instituted enquiries and found that Ed. Leighton, a notorious safe breaker, had possessed a brother, and the description of this brother coincided absolutely with that of Charles Alden. Here was the reason for Alden's obvious hatred when he had spoken about the 'Phantom Slayer,' for the unknown criminal had done his brother to death on a lonely part of the Portsmouth Road, and taken from him the pearl necklace that he had stolen, with much ingenuity, from Lady Bradbury.

Blackmore had said nothing to the girl about his discovery, for he was convinced that she was ignorant of the fact that Alden had not been her husband's real name, and nothing was to be gained by undeceiving her. Also his enquiries had led him to the conclusion that the dead man, if not actually a crook, had not been as straight as he might be. Several of the papers in the bank safe had dealt with deals in which he had been concerned that were not strictly on the square. Blackmore was certain, however, that his wife had known nothing about these transactions and decided to keep them to himself. But all this had done nothing to help him one iota with the main issue, the running to earth of the 'Phantom Slayer,' for though he had probed and questioned and set on foot countless enquiries he had failed to elicit anything regarding Alden's intimate friends, or succeeded in obtaining the slightest clue to the name of the man who had been with him at Evesham Mansions, who, according to his statement, was also aware of the true identity of the elusive killer.

John had to admit himself beaten — for the time being at any rate — and this was the state of affairs when, on the morning of the fifth day he learned from Kenton that the Hugh Ascot flat in Portman Square had been broken into during the night and the famous Ascot emeralds stolen.

The inspector had dropped in shortly after breakfast to see if Blackmore had any fresh news, and had acquainted his friend with the details of the robbery.

'We've got the fellow who did it,' he concluded rubbing vigorously at his moustache. 'Caught him red-handed leaving the place with the stuff. You know him, Peter Hinton.'

' 'Peter the Piper,' eh?' said Blackmore interestedly. 'He's been quiet for some time now.'

'Yes,' Kenton grunted. 'He got up to his old tricks all right last night, lived well up to his nickname. Got into the flat by swarming up a drain pipe at the back that you wouldn't have thought a cat could climb. He'd have got away too, only he slipped coming down and broke his leg. It was hard luck on Peter but lucky for us.'

Blackmore scarcely heard him. Into his eyes crept a strange gleam, and a peculiar little smile curved the corners of his lips.

'By Jove! it's a chance!' he exclaimed suddenly, and the inspector and Cartwright looked at him in astonishment.

'What's a chance?' grunted Kenton. 'I don't know what you're talking about.'

'You will in a minute,' said Blackmore, rising to his feet and lighting a cigarette. 'Where have you taken Hinton?'

'He's in the infirmary,' said Kenton. 'At Cannon Row. Why?'

'Have you given out to the papers that he's been arrested?' said John without answering his question, and the inspector shook his head.

'No,' he replied. 'It was too late for the morning editions, I expect it will be in the evening ones though.'

'It won't,' answered Blackmore. 'Listen, Kenton. The fact that 'Peter the Piper' has been arrested has got to be suppressed. You can give out an account of the robbery with full particulars, but you've got to say that the man succeeded in getting away with the emeralds.'

'What on earth for?' spluttered Kenton in amazement.

'Because I'm going to take Peter Hinton's place,' said Blackmore quietly.

'Great Scott!' exclaimed Cartwright as a light broke on him. 'I understand what you're getting at.'

'Oh, do you,' snapped the puzzled inspector. 'Well, then, it's a jolly sight more than I do. Perhaps you wouldn't mind explaining?'

'Certainly I'll explain,' answered Blackmore with a faint smile. 'The Ascot emeralds are well known, and their value is considerable. If the fact they have been stolen is announced in the papers and that the thief got away, it's almost certain to attract the attention of the 'Phantom Slayer.' The method by which the burglar gained access will stamp the robbery as being the work of 'Peter the Piper' and in all probability our unknown friend will at once try and get into communication with him in the usual manner. You see now?'

The Scotland Yard man jumped to his feet.

'Of course,' he exclaimed. 'If he tries to make an appointment you'll keep it, disguised as Hinton?'

'Exactly,' replied Blackmore quietly. 'It's a chance, but it may come off, unless he's got scared and decides to rest on his laurels.'

'It'll be horrible risky,' said the secretary anxiously. 'Supposing he does swallow the bait, and recognises you?'

Blackmore shrugged his shoulders.

'I shall have to be prepared for that. If anything does come of my plan I propose to let you and Kenton know the place and time of the appointment, so that you can both be present. If he does deliver himself into our hands we won't take any chances of him slipping through our fingers.'

'It's a good idea,' said the inspector approvingly. 'If I can use your telephone I can get straight on to the Yard now and arrange for Peter's arrest to be kept quiet.'

'Do,' said John, 'and also get in touch with Hugh Ascot and explain to him that for certain reasons it is necessary for an announcement to appear that the robbery was successful. While you're doing that I'll get some things together that I shall need, and as soon as you've finished we'll go to Cannon Row and interview 'Peter the Piper.''

Detective-Inspector Kenton crossed to the telephone, and Blackmore went upstairs to his bedroom. By the time he returned, clad in his overcoat, and carrying a suitcase, the inspector had concluded his telephoning. He turned from the instrument as John re-entered.

'I've been speaking to the Assistant Commissioner,' he said, 'and he is arranging everything. He thinks it's an excellent plan.'

'And to Hugh Ascot?' enquired Blackmore.

Kenton snorted.

'He was a bit difficult at first,' he grumbled. 'Said he didn't like the notoriety or some such nonsense, but I managed to talk him round, and promised I'd call and explain everything this afternoon.'

'Good,' said John. 'Then we might as well be getting along.'

Fifteen minutes later they arrived at Cannon Row, which is practically a part of Scotland Yard, and were conducted by a sergeant into the small, whitewashed ward that is used to house prisoners whose ill-health precludes them from occupying the ordinary cells. There was only one patient in the place. He lay in the farthest of the half dozen little truckle beds. A thin, hollow-cheeked, rat of a man, whose shifty eyes looked at them suspiciously as they entered.

Blackmore laid the suitcase he had brought with him on a table and approached the bed, standing for some seconds gazing down at this man intently, then he looked up at Kenton.

'Where are his clothes?' he asked.

The inspector consulted the sergeant who retired to a large cupboard and presently returned with an arm full of garments which he deposited on the chair by the side of the table. John opened the suitcase and took out a large mirror, a black-japanned metal box, several jars and bottles, and a number of wigs. He set up the mirror and lifting the case on to the floor, proceeded to arrange the contents methodically on the table. The man in the bed eyed him curiously as he made these preparations.

'What's the game?' he enquired at last, in a voice that held a strong tinge of Cockney in its tone.

'You'll see very shortly,' said John, as, divesting himself of collar and tie, coat and waistcoat, he seated himself before the mirror.

John Blackmore was a past master in the difficult art of disguise, and used as he was to his friend's ability in this direction, Inspector Kenton looked on in wonderment as he commenced to make-up. The stage lost a great actor when John Blackmore joined the police force. Swiftly and surely his hands moved among the collection of bottles and paints in front of him. An application from a jar of cosmetic gave to his face the peculiar sallow tint of the man in the bed. A tiny piece of wax in each nostril transformed his nose, altering its shape to the broad, rather squat organ of 'Peter the Piper.' Raising his eyes every now and again to shoot a quick glance at his model John proceeded swiftly with his metamorphosis. A line here and there, drawn with a deft touch of the artist, and the character of John Blackmore disappeared, and in its place there took shape a facsimile of 'Peter the Piper,' so like, that it might have been his twin brother who sat at the table. Selecting a wig of the exact colour of the crook's hair John adjusted it on his head, carefully sticking it in place with spirit gum, and when he had trimmed it and brushed it in the way Hinton did his hair the transformation was complete. It was no longer Blackmore, but Peter Hinton who rose from the chair and donned the clothing which the sergeant had laid out in readiness.

'Well, I'll be damned!' ejaculated Kenton. 'It's wonderful. One of the best things you've ever done.' He looked from John to the man on the bed. 'Why, even his own mother couldn't tell the difference.'

'I think it will pass,' said Blackmore

examining himself critically in the mirror.

'So that's the idea, eh,' muttered Peter. 'Going to impersonate me, are you? Well, I don't know what you blooming well think you're doing, nothing to gain by it.'

Without answering him John turned to Kenton.

'There was nothing in any of these pockets,' he said. 'I suppose he was searched when he was arrested? Have you got the contents?'

Again the sergeant went to the cupboard and came back with a shallow tray on which reposed a watch, a cigarette case, a small bunch of keys and a wallet. Blackmore picked up the keys and looked at them.

'What's his address?' he asked the inspector.

Kenton withdrew a bulky notebook from his pocket and consulted it.

'Sixteen Primrose Buildings, Gray's Inn Road,' he answered. 'It's a block of flats near the Holborn end.'

John nodded.

'I suppose this is the key of the front door?' He addressed 'Peter the Piper,' and indicated a Yale key on the bunch in his hand.

The crook looked at him, his small eyes narrowed to slits.

'No good my telling you it isn't,' he replied. 'It wouldn't take you long to find out, and I'd blooming well like to know what you're going to do.'

'In all probability one of the things I'm going to do is to save your life,' answered John. 'You can thank your stars you were caught last night, Hinton. You're safe here, and that's more than you would have been if you'd got away. The 'Phantom Slayer' is dangerous to argue with.'

Peter's jaw dropped.

'The 'Phantom Slayer!'' he replied. 'Blimey! Do you think he'd have gone after me?'

'With the Ascot emeralds at stake, I most certainly do,' replied Blackmore. 'Instead of which, I'm going after him.'

'I see the wheeze,' said 'Peter the Piper,' his quick brain suddenly grasping the reason for John's impersonation. 'Well, I wish you luck, and I 'ope you get him, the dirty tyke.'

'I hope so too,' answered Blackmore grimly as he turned away.

He replaced the things he had brought in the suitcase together with his own clothes and handed it over to Cartwright. The secretary had been, for him, strangely silent, watching his employer's preparations without a word. His heart was filled with a vague sense of dread, without, however, being able to give it a tangible name. It was true that Blackmore was running a considerable risk by taking the place of Peter Hinton, but it was not nearly so grave as many he had taken before in the course of his adventures. Yet Cartwright could not put aside the feeling of intense depression that had come over him — a feeling of impending disaster.

They left the ward, and in the big charge room John took leave of Kenton and the secretary.

'If anything occurs,' he said, 'I'll phone the Yard.'

He left them and took a bus to Holborn. It didn't take him long to find Primrose Buildings, and even less time to find the flat he sought. 'Peter the Piper's' abode was on the fifth floor, and as he inserted the key into the grimy front door he experienced a little thrill of excitement. Would the chance he had taken bear fruit or was the 'Phantom Slayer' too wary to risk another coup so soon after the murder of Falkner.

Blackmore was inclined to think that the bait of the Ascot emeralds would draw him. After all, from the unknown murderer's point of view there was very little danger to himself, and the series of past successes would give him confidence. Like all criminals, his predominating characteristic was vanity; he showed this in a dozen ways. It was just this very vanity that Blackmore counted on, having eluded detection for so long he was, in all probability steeped in a supreme self-confidence, a conviction that his brain was cleverer than those who had set out to track him down. And Blackmore was hoping that this conceit would lead to his undoing.

These thoughts crossed his mind as he crossed into the tiny passage of 'Peter the

Piper's' flat and carefully closed the door behind him.

A greater contrast to the rather sordid exterior it would have been difficult to find. The crook had apparently his own ideas of comfort and carried them out effectually, for the hall was luxuriant, even if a trifle crude in its furnishing. Having taken off his hat, which he hung on the carved oak hall stand, Blackmore proceeded leisurely to take stock of the whole place.

Leading from the lobby were two doors, one on either side. Turning the handle of the door on the right he walked in to a small apartment furnished as a sitting room. The chairs that flanked the hearth were deep and comfortable, and the rest of the room was in accord, even if the colour scheme was a trifle startling. Going out into the hall again he crossed to the room on the other side. This, as he had supposed, proved to be a bedroom. This also was elaborately furnished. The walnut suite was a good quality, and the bed, in oxodized silver, looked comfortable. Opening off the bedroom was a small bathroom, the fittings of which left nothing to be desired.

Blackmore decided that his stay would at any rate be under pleasant conditions. A further exploration unearthed a kitchenette at the end of the hall. The larder was well stocked, and realising that he was beginning to feel hungry John prepared himself a light lunch, made some coffee and returned with it to the sitting room. Having eaten his meal he lit a cigarette and settling down in one of the easy chairs with a book that he found on a side-table, proceeded to wait developments.

The afternoon passed slowly into evening, and John roused himself from his thoughts, for he had long since discarded the book as being unreadable, and went along to the kitchen to make some tea. He was carrying the tray back along the passage when the letter box clicked. He deposited his burden on the table in the sitting room and returned to see what it was. Evidently Peter Hinton had his newspapers delivered, two evening editions reposed on the mat by the front door. Blackmore opened them while he sipped his tea, and chuckled as he read the account of the robbery at Portman Square, which was splashed on the front page.

Kenton had done his work well, for there was no mention of the fact that the thief had been caught, and anyone reading the affair would have concluded that he had got clean away with the jewels.

The evening brought nothing except boredom. By the time John had decided to turn in for an early night's rest he was heartily sick of his enforced vigil. He was asleep almost as soon as his head touched the pillow, and it was broad daylight before he opened his eyes again. He discovered from the clock by the bedside that it was a quarter to eight. He rose, bathed, and was cooking his breakfast when a rat-tat-tat announced the arrival of the postman. He hurried out of the little kitchen to the front door. There were three letters, and his pulses beat a trifle faster than usual as he stooped and picked them up. Two were obviously bills or circulars, from the halfpenny stamp, but the third was a common, white vanilla envelope, and the name and address was typewritten.

Blackmore's eyes gleamed as he tore it open for he had noted the chipped P and the E slightly out of alignment that characterised the communications from the 'Phantom Slayer.'

9

The Phantom Slayer

The note inside was brief and to the point and began without preliminary.

'To save you the trouble of attempting to dispose of the Ascot emeralds elsewhere I will make you an offer for them. Be at the old well by Cæsar's Camp on Wimbledon Common at one o'clock precisely tomorrow night, bringing the jewels with you.'

There followed the usual threat of exposure to the police unless the writer's demands were complied with.

Blackmore folded the single sheet of paper and put it thoughtfully in his pocket. His shot in the dark had turned out successfully after all, and he had not been wrong in his belief that the 'Phantom Slayer' would make a bid to get hold of the Ascot emeralds. The place chosen for the meeting he knew well, that dark and lonely spot in the coppice of pine trees in the very centre of the vast track of common land which was supposed to be an old camping place used by Julius Cæsar in the ages gone by. A beautiful spot indeed for a crime such as had made the reputation of the 'Phantom Slayer.'

As soon as he had finished his breakfast Blackmore left Primrose Buildings and hurried along Gray's Inn Road in search of a public telephone, for he wanted to acquaint Cartwright of the latest development and also give his secretary the instructions for that night, for he had no intention of keeping the appointment alone. He was determined that this time there should be no chance of the 'Phantom Slayer' slipping through his fingers, and was going to lay his plans accordingly.

He kept a sharp look-out as he walked briskly up the street to see if there was anyone following him, for it was quite possible that the 'Slayer' might decide to keep a watch on his victim. But he saw no one who looked in the least suspicious.

He took the precaution, however, of stopping at the tobacco shop to buy some cigarettes and chatted for some time with the proprietor. When he left the shop he paused in the doorway and lighted one of the cigarettes, looking about meanwhile to see if any one of the few passers by were still in the immediate neighbourhood, for he had given them all plenty of time to get well out of sight. If there was anybody shadowing him they would still be loitering about to see him come out, but none of the people who had been in the vicinity when he went in were still there, and John was satisfied.

He found a call office a few yards further on and giving the Mecklinburg Square number was soon in close conversation with his secretary.

'I want you to get in touch with Kenton,' he said after he had told Harry of the arrival of the letter. 'Tell him to bring a couple of plain clothes men with him and be at Cæsar's Camp at five minutes to one. You know where it is, don't you.'

Cartwright replied in the affirmative.

'Good,' said John. 'You'd better go along, too, only whatever you do, don't get there before five minutes to one. Our friend may be there early on the watch, and if he sees anything suspicious we can say goodbye to all chance of catching him.'

After a few more instructions concerning some letters that had arrived in his absence John rang off.

As he strolled back up the Gray's Inn Road he tried to make up his mind how he should spend the day. It was early and there were many hours to fill in before nightfall, the time of his appointment. Blackmore felt disinclined to go back to Hinton's flat. For one thing, it would be awkward if any friends of the crook's called and started talking about something that he — John — was in total ignorance of, a possibility that had occurred to him on the previous day, and for another, the prospect of being shut up in the stuffy abode was not in the least an appealing one.

He decided at length that he would fill in his time by paying a visit to the scene of his forthcoming meeting with the 'Phantom Slayer.'

Wimbledon Common was one of the beauty spots of London, and a walk across the broad expanse would do him good. He had no sooner made up his mind than he started to put the plan into execution. Boarding a bus at Holborn he was swiftly carried to Waterloo, and from thence, by the electric railway to Wimbledon Station. A short walk brought him to the outskirts of the Common and with his pipe gripped between his teeth Blackmore set off in the direction of Cæsar's Camp.

The day was perfect, with a sharp snap in the air, and the thickly-clustered silver birch trees with which the Common abounded looked lovely in their autumnal beauty, the slender white of their trunks silhouetted against the browns and reds of the fading foliage. There was not a soul about, and in the silence of the wood John was able to give himself up to the enjoyment of his solitary ramble. For the moment he forgot the dark and sinister business on which he was engaged, for town dweller though he was, he loved the country, with all its changing moods and scenes, and in Autumn.

Presently he came to Cæsar's Camp and stood for some time gazing at the old well, now filled with rubble and stones almost to the brim. It was an ideal place for the 'Phantom Slayer's' purpose, for it was a considerable distance from any main thoroughfare, and although a fairly broad road ran some few hundred yards away, it was seldom if ever used, except during the summer by picnic parties and the like, and at the hour chosen for the interview would be as deserted and far from human ken as if it were in the middle of the Sahara Desert.

For the rest of the day Blackmore roamed about the country, taking a belated lunch at a small wayside public house, and it was not until dusk was falling that he returned to Gray's Inn Road, feeling all the better for his day's outing both in mind and body.

He was healthily tired after his long walk and after making a cup of tea stretched himself out on the settee in the sitting room for a rest before setting out to keep his appointment.

At half past ten he rose, washed, ate some supper and putting on an overcoat of Hinton's and a cloth cap, took a last look round before leaving the flat for good. As he closed the front door behind him and descended the narrow stone stairway he felt a little thrill of elation pass through him. The long chase was nearing its end now, and a few hours should see finish written to the 'Phantom Slayer's' activities.

Twelve o'clock was striking as he got out of the train at Wimbledon Station, and he swung off briskly in the direction of the Common. He had a long walk in front of him before he reached his destination, and he judged that he would arrive at Cæsar's Camp about a quarter to one.

The Common looked bleak and uninviting, a cold wind had sprung up and was blowing in fitful gusts across the wide expanse, and John pulled up the collar of his overcoat as he struck off along a narrow pathway that led into the heart of the woods. It was pitch dark and he was more than once on the point of losing his way. The landmarks he had noted on his visit earlier in the day were, in most cases, indistinguishable, or so altered in appearance that he failed to recognise them. However, by the occasional use of his torch he managed to keep a fairly straight course, and presently found himself on the broad stretch of road that ran within a few hundred yards of the place he was seeking.

He wondered which way Cartwright and Kenton would come, and concluded that it would, in all probability, be by this same road, for it would be impossible for anyone to come by way of the woods unless they were acquainted with every inch of the ground; there was not even a footpath to guide them.

He reached the camp sooner than he expected, glancing at his watch as he approached the old well he saw that it was barely twenty minutes to one; he had some time to wait. He looked round him, even in the daylight it was a miserable enough place, but in the dark —

Iron nerved as he was, he couldn't

prevent a little shiver passing through him, the pines seemed to brood over the spot like living sentinels, shrouding it in shadows of palpable black, while their branches whispered ceaselessly in the rising wind with a sound like the surge of the sea, and at the same time there hung over all a profound and enveloping silence.

He paced up and down, stopping every now and again to listen intently, his hand gripping the squat butt of the automatic, but everything was still, save for the wind in the trees there was not a sound. The minutes dragged slowly by. It must be getting on for five minutes to one, he thought, but there was no sign of Cartwright and the inspector. Perhaps they had already arrived and were concealed somewhere among the many patches of gorse that surrounded the little coppice. That his secretary would be on time he was certain, he knew that so much depended on it.

A faint sound from the direction of the roadway caused him to stop, his body stiffening into alertness, it was the sound of a footfall. The noise was repeated nearer, somebody was coming towards him, stumbling over the rough ground. Blackmore strained his eyes to pierce the intense darkness, but he could see nothing. Nearer and nearer came the footsteps and now he was able to distinguish a shadowy figure approaching through the scattered pine trees — a darker smudge of black against the black of the night.

In spite of his usual calmness his heart throbbed in his breast with excitement, for it could only be the 'Phantom Slayer.' As the man — for man it was — drew closer, a sudden blinding ray of light leaped out of the darkness and focused itself upon John. The bright glare prevented him being able to distinguish anything of the person who held the torch, but presently a voice spoke from behind the light.

'Hinton?' it said, in a husky whisper.

'Yes,' answered John and his voice so closely resembled that of the man he was impersonating that it was impossible to detect the difference.

'Good!' said the 'Phantom Slayer.' The beam from his torch still played on the detective's face and John sensed the close scrutiny with which he was being regarded. 'Well, we may as well get to business, eh?' continued the husky voice, after a pause. 'Did you bring the stones with you?'

'Yes,' said John again.

'How much do you want for them?'

'Five thousand isn't a lot to ask,' Blackmore muttered.

'No, but it's a lot to get,' retorted the other. There was a click and the torch went out. 'I'll give you a hundred — cash.'

Blackmore could see his man now. He was dressed in a heavy motor coat that fell almost to his heels, and his face was concealed in some sort of mask, with mica eyepieces resembling goggles; this accounted for the husky, muffled tone of his voice.

'A hundred?' John echoed and laughed harshly. 'What do you take me for, a blooming philanthropist?'

'I take you for a sensible man,'

answered the 'Phantom Slayer.' 'A hundred is better than nothing.'

'But I can easily get five thousand for the emeralds,' began John.

'Can you?' snapped the masked man, and as if by magic there appeared in his hand a squat, curiously shaped pistol. 'Listen to me, my friend. I want those jewels and I mean to have them, if you like to take my offer, all well and good, if you don't — well, I shall take them for nothing, that's all.'

John was silent for a moment, his keen brain working at express speed. Cartwright and Kenton should be somewhere near at hand if they had carried out his instructions, and in a second or two would be due to put in an appearance and —

'Well?' said the 'Phantom Slayer' impatiently. 'Have you made up your mind?'

John's hand closed on the butt of his pistol and he thumbed down the safety catch.

'Yes,' he repeated. 'I'm not selling at that price!'

'Very well — then take what's coming to you.'

The masked man raised his arm and John, guessing his intention, whipped his automatic from his pocket and took a step forward, but his foot caught in a rut in the uneven ground and he went sprawling. The shock of his fall sent the pistol spinning out of his hand. Before he could attempt to recover himself the 'Phantom Slayer' was bending over him and he felt the gas pistol thrust into his face. The thought flashed through his brain that somehow or other Cartwright and the inspector had failed him, he must act on his own account. As the unknown murderer pressed the trigger John shut his eyes and held his breath. He felt the released gas strike his face with almost the force of a blow, and at the same moment rolled over, clutching at the ground with his fingers.

After one or two spasmodic movements he allowed his muscles to relax and lay still. There was a pause and then he was turned roughly over. Through his lowered lids he saw the dark figure of his assailant bending over him. The 'Phantom Slayer' unfastened his overcoat and began rapidly to search his pockets. John smiled inwardly as presently, with a grunt of satisfaction, the masked man located the packet of sham jewellery that he had prepared and placed in his breast pocket.

He straightened up and examined it for a second in the light of his torch, then slipping it into the pocket of his overcoat and without a backward glance at his supposed victim he made off swiftly in the direction of whence he had come.

No sooner had he vanished in the darkness than John was on his feet, and noiseless and silent as a shadow, began to follow in his wake. Making his way through the fringe of pine he walked quickly across the common until he came to the roadway. It was lighter here away from the shadow of the trees, and Blackmore saw that a large, closed car, its lights extinguished, was drawn up by the side of the broad track. The man in the mask was going towards this, and John realised that unless he could do something quickly he was in danger of losing him altogether. Unarmed as he was it was useless attempting to tackle him single-handed, for in addition to the gas pistol he would, in all probability, carry a revolver. There had been no time for John to look for his own weapon. If only Cartwright and Kenton had been there.

He racked his brain to try and think of some way out of the difficulty. The 'Phantom Slayer' was barely fifty yards from the car and in another moment or so would be driving off. The rough ground sloped in a deep declivity to the road, and John saw that a thick clump of gorse bushes ran almost down to the place where the car was standing. If he could reach the machine first there was just a chance that he might be able, somehow, to hang on the back and thus still keep track of the man after all.

Dropping down under cover of the bushes he wormed his way on all fours down the bank, and found himself within two yards of the back of the car. His eyes gleamed with satisfaction as he saw that it was fitted with a luggage carrier. The masked man had already reached the limousine and was getting in. A second later the lights were switched on and John saw that it was a high powered Spange, the latest make. It suddenly occurred to him to leave some sort of sign for Cartwright and Kenton in case anything had delayed them and they arrived later. Hastily feeling in his pocket he found a pencil, but he hadn't a scrap of paper on him. Then he remembered that he had slipped a packet of cigarettes in his overcoat before leaving Gray's Inn Road.

The 'Phantom Slayer' had already started the engine as John tore open the cardboard carton and tipped the cigarettes out on to the ground. In feverish haste he scribbled a few lines, writing by touch, for he could not see in the dark, signed his name and stuck it on a projecting twig.

The car moved forward and was gathering speed when he left his place of concealment, and running after it managed to grip the carrier and pull it down. The man seated at the wheel drove on through the night, unconscious of the fact that he was carrying a passenger in the shape of the man he had left behind for dead, unconscious also that Hinton cloaked the identity of John Blackmore!

10

The Chase

When Cartwright had received his employer's telephone message from Gray's Inn Road that morning informing him of the 'Phantom Slayer's' communication, he had lost no time in hurrying round to Scotland Yard and acquainting Inspector Kenton with the news. Together they had discussed the arrangements for the evening, and it had been decided that Kenton should pick Harry up at Mecklinburg Square. John had been emphatic that they should not arrive at the place appointed for the meeting before five minutes to one, so they had fixed twelve o'clock as the hour to start, giving themselves, as they believed, ample time.

After consulting a map of the district Cartwright suggested that since they were travelling by car the best route to take would be that through Putney, reaching

Wimbledon Common via Putney Heath. The roads were less frequented this way, and just before reaching the Portsmouth Road there was a broad track marked in the map that ran across the Common within a few hundred yards of their objective — Cæsar's Camp.

Harry's idea was that they should leave the car some distance down the road and go the rest of the way on foot. Having settled all the details with the inspector he returned to Mecklinburg Square to fill in the day as best he could, until it was time to start on the excursion to Wimbledon.

The vague sense of depression that had come over him ever since Blackmore had mentioned his plans of impersonating 'Peter the Piper' was, if anything, deeper than ever. Try as he would, he couldn't shake it off and as the hours went by his uneasiness increased.

He tried to distract his mind with a book, after lunch, but found that it was impossible to concentrate on the printed pages. He found himself reading the same sentence over and over again, without any idea as to its meaning. He gave it up in despair at last, and throwing the book down crossed over to his desk and sought relief from the feeling of foreboding by emerging himself in work.

There were several days' cuttings to be classified and letters to be filed, but after an hour's fruitless effort he discovered that he had got Bs mixed up with Ms and Cs with O. He gave this up too, and throwing himself into a chair gazed at the fire, allowing his gloomy thoughts full play. Exactly what it was that was worrying him he couldn't decide, it was just an intangible premonition of approaching disaster, a dull leaden weight that seemed to be on the pit of his stomach, and a cold sensation as of icy fingers about his heart. He was convinced that Blackmore's meeting with the 'Phantom Slayer' was going to lead to danger.

Looked at in the cold light of reason there seemed to be no justification for this conviction. He and Kenton, together with the two plain clothes policemen would be present at the interview; so as far as he could see nothing could possibly happen, but all the same the little whispering voice of warning would not be silenced. At last it became so unbearable sitting still that he put on his hat and coat and went out.

For some time he walked aimlessly about, up one street and down another, and presently, finding that he was outside a brilliantly lighted cinema he went in and bought a seat. The picture was a good one, but when he came out Cartwright for the life of him couldn't have said what it was all about.

It was getting late as he strolled back in the direction of Mecklinburg Square, and with a sigh of thankfulness realised that it would shortly be time for Kenton to arrive and start on their expedition to Cæsar's Camp.

The day had been endless, one of the longest he had ever spent, he was glad that it was nearly over. Twelve o'clock came at last, and a few minutes after a thunderous knock sounded on the front door. Harry opened it, the bulky figure of Detective Inspector Kenton, muffled up in a heavy overcoat, stood on the step and behind him, drawn up at the kerb, a police car with two men seated on the front seat.

'Are you ready?' jerked Kenton, tugging at his moustache impatiently.

'I shall be in a second,' answered Harry. 'Wait a minute.'

He struggled into his overcoat, hurried into the study, and dragging open a drawer in the desk took out an automatic. Examining it quickly to see if the mechanism was in order he slipped it into his pocket, together with a supply of cartridges, and rejoined the inspector at the door. In less than two minutes they were speeding away on the first part of their journey to Cæsar's Camp.

The car was a powerful one, and considering the amount of traffic in Piccadilly and the Fulham Palace Road they made good going. Half past twelve was striking as they reached the foot of Putney Hill, the steep incline up which, eight months previously, Lew Steen walked to his death. They breasted the slope and turning sharply to the right at the top by the A.A. man's box swung off along the lonely road that crosses the heath.

'We shall be in plenty of time,' said Kenton, with satisfaction. 'We'll do it nicely.'

Cartwright nodded.

'Another ten minutes should bring us to the branch road leading to the camp,' he replied. 'It's a fair distance, even then, but I should think it would be safe to go a good way along by car. They were running down the hill that gives on to the Portsmouth Road as he spoke and as they came again to the flat the car suddenly began to slow down.

'What are you stopping for?' snapped Kenton, leaning forward and speaking to the driver. 'What's the matter?'

'Don't know, sir,' the man replied, turning his head. 'Something seems to have gone wrong with the engine.'

The rhythmic note of the motor had changed to a jerky staccato mutter and then, without warning, the car stopped altogether.

'For God's sake don't stop!' cried Cartwright.

'Can't help it.' The driver flung open the door and hastily got down. 'Something pretty serious has happened.' He ran round to the bonnet and lifting the side peered at the engine by the aid of a torch. After a short while he looked up. 'The oil pipe lubricating the piston shaft has broken,' he said. 'We've been running dry most of the way, I expect it's the big end that's gone, that's the cause of the trouble.'

'Can't you get the thing to move at all?' said Harry in an agony of apprehension.

'I'll try. But if the big end's gone and got jammed in the crank case it's hopeless,' said the driver dubiously.

He tried again and again to get the engine to start but without result. At last he turned a perspiring face to Kenton and the secretary.

'I'm afraid it's no good,' he said. 'We shall have to go the rest of the way on foot.'

'We shan't get there on time,' cried Kenton. 'It must be a quarter to one now.'

Harry's heart sank, his vague foreboding of disaster had become a real and tangible one.

They were a good two miles from their

destination and in the middle of that dark and lonely waste John Blackmore was waiting to meet one of the most desperate criminals it had ever been his lot to come up against, and he was waiting — alone.

'Come on!' exclaimed Harry, as the thought stirred him into action. 'It's no good wasting time.'

He leaped out of the car and went racing along the road without waiting to see if the others were following or not. Luckily the car had broken down close to the turning that led across the Common to Cæsar's Camp, and as he swung round the sharp bend he heard the heavy footfalls of Inspector Kenton pounding along in his rear. They grew fainter as he sped on, his arms pressed to his side and his mind filled with one idea — not to fail his employer.

The road was scarcely a racing track, and again and again Harry stumbled and almost fell as his feet caught in the deep holes that pitted the surface, but he kept on. He must have covered a considerable distance when suddenly, far ahead, he saw a red light flash out. He knew it at once for the pale lamp of a car, and almost at the same instant the faint hum of a powerful engine was borne to his ears. Gathering every ounce of his strength Cartwright put on a spurt. The light in front grew brighter as he raced on. He was able to make out the vague outline of a number plate hazily in the white beam that shone across it. He was still too far off to see the number and then when he was scarcely two hundred yards away the light began to move, slowly at first, and then faster and faster as the car evidently gathered speed. All at once it went out for a second, then flashed on again, growing smaller and dimmer, and then faded into the darkness.

Cartwright came up to the place where the car had been standing and stopped, gasping and breathless. To whom had it belonged? He answered the question almost before it entered his mind. It must have belonged to the 'Phantom Slayer,' no one else was likely to have been at the spot at such an hour, then what had happened to Blackmore?

He looked about him in the blackness, listening intently, but no sound broke the stillness of the night except the sighing of the wind in the trees. He felt a wave of physical sickness pass over him. Was Blackmore lying somewhere near lifeless and still, another victim of the unknown murderer? Had the breakdown of their car cost him his life?

Taking his electric torch from his pocket he flashed its white light on the roadway. The marks where the car had stood were plainly visible, and a little pool of black oil showed that it had been there for some time. He directed the light further afield to the side of the road. A straggling clump of gorse bushes grew close by and the beam gleamed on something white stuck among them.

He saw that it was a piece of cardboard and was almost passing it by when he noticed, scattered at the base of the bush, a dozen or more unused cigarettes. The origin of the piece of card flashed through his mind, and with a rapidly beating heart he looked at it. It was covered with an irregular pencilled scrawl, which he found difficulty in deciphering:

'Spange car. YE 27093. On back. Follow. J.B.'

The flood of relief that poured through him made Cartwright tremble and he almost dropped the card. So Blackmore was still alive after all.

The sound of hurriedly approaching feet caused him to turn. Inspector Kenton came up, puffing and blowing like a grampus. Harry showed him the message and told him of the car he had seen drive off.

'How the devil can we follow?' spluttered the inspector, mopping his streaming face with his handkerchief. 'It must be miles away by now.'

'We can but try,' said Cartwright. 'This road runs in practically a straight line until it joins the main road into Wimbledon. When we reach that there's a chance we shall pass a policeman on duty who saw the car pass.'

He set off at a brisk pace, followed by the panting Kenton. Presently they arrived at the place where the roads intersected. There was no policeman, but a little way along the road was under repair and Kenton questioned the night watchman.

'Yes, I saw a large motor go by some half an hour ago,' he replied, slowly scratching his head. 'It were going pretty fast too, — and there was a feller 'anging on the back. What I'd like to know is — '

'Come on, Kenton,' exclaimed Harry, cutting him short.

They had just started to hurry off again when they saw a small car coming towards them and acting on a sudden impulse Cartwright stepped into the middle of the road and held out his arms. With a grinding of brakes the machine came to a standstill.

'What the dickens do you think you're playing at?' raved an angry voice indignantly.

Cartwright walked round to the side of the little two-seater. The driver was a young man with a fat red face and he glared at the secretary with a pair of large pale blue eyes. Although the soft hat he was wearing completely concealed his hair Cartwright felt that he would have been disappointed if it had been any other colour than bright orange.

'I'm sorry to pull you up,' he apologised, 'but it is urgent.'

He launched into a short explanation before he could be interrupted, the stout man's eyes growing larger and larger as he proceeded.

'Gee!' he ejaculated, when Harry had finished. 'And you want to use my car to follow this Johnny?'

'If you don't mind,' said the secretary politely.

'Mind?' the owner of the car shot out the word with the force of a small explosion. 'My dear fellow, you couldn't have done me a better turn, I wouldn't have missed it for the world. I've been bored stiff for days and this is a miracle, jump in.' He opened the door invitingly. 'There's a dicky seat,' he said looking at Kenton. 'Would you mind pulling it open?'

The inspector grunted an affirmative, and raising the cover clambered laboriously into the back.

'Right ho!' said the driver as soon as he

was in. 'Then we're off.'

He rammed in the gear lever and the car shot along with a jerk that caused Kenton to clutch frantically at the back of the front seat, and gathering speed at every turn of the wheel, tore down the road towards Wimbledon.

The pursuit of the 'Phantom Slayer' had begun!

11

A Fiendish Plan

It was anything but comfortable clinging precariously to the narrow luggage carrier, but Blackmore managed to hang on, despite the fact that he was continually being thrown and bumped about as the car sped over the uneven ground. As to their ultimate destination, he hadn't the least idea, but he was determined that having found his man he would stick to him until he learnt his identity. He knew that he would never get such an opportunity again, and if he lost him now it might be months before he would be able to get on his track a second time — if ever.

He was puzzled and a little anxious to account for Cartwright and Kenton's non-appearance on the scene. His instructions had been explicit and it was unlike his secretary to fail him at such a crucial moment; something must have happened to prevent him getting to Cæsar's Camp at the time stipulated, and although he thought of several reasons the true one never dawned on him until he had swung out of the narrow turning and was racing down the main road on the way to Wimbledon. And then like a flash the possibility of the car having broken down occurred to him.

Of course that must be the only reason, he thought, and if it were the case Cartwright would make all haste to get to the spot arranged as fast as he could.

He wondered if his message would be found, if it was he knew his secretary would lose no time in trying to pick up the trail of the car, the number and description of which he, John, had left behind. It shouldn't be impossible to trace, for even if the number was a false one, which in all probability it was, the Spange was an expensive car and there were few of them on the road. At the same time it would not be by any means an easy task and John began to cast round in his mind for some means by which he could indicate to Cartwright the route they were taking.

Slitting into a receptacle beside the carrier on which he was crouched was a tin of petrol and another of lubricating oil. As his eyes fell upon the latter he was suddenly struck with an idea, it might not be any good at all, but at least it was worth trying, and Cartwright was a brainy fellow. Leaning to one side he managed, with considerable difficulty, to detach the tin from its fastening. As he had hoped, it was a full one and contained the thick, black oil used for lubricating the crank case. He unscrewed the cap and clinging on to the car with his right hand, tilted the can with his left, and at regular intervals allowed a dollop of the treacly liquid to fall on to the roadway.

If Cartwright was trailing him and saw these drops of oil at equal distances apart he felt sure that he would guess the reason, and if he did it was almost as good as if John had left signposts all the way.

They had reached Wimbledon by now and as they sped on past the station he saw the policeman on point duty at the crossings turn and stare after the great car as it thundered by. The man had evidently seen him perched on the carrier. A short distance farther on the car veered sharply to the right, going in the direction of Earlsfield, and in a remarkably short time, considering the distance, it roared through the little suburb and continued on towards Clapham, passing the junction and turning into Wandsworth Road.

There was no sign of slowing down, and John began to feel sick and cramped from his uncomfortable position on the back. Where were they making for, he thought? Apparently somewhere in the east, for presently they passed the Elephant and Castle and proceeded on down the Borough.

John began to consider the advisability of signalling the next policeman they came to, and having the car stopped, but he rejected the idea almost before it entered his brain. The 'Phantom Slayer' was a desperate man, and it would take more than himself and one policeman to stop him, and the result of such a move might be to lose him altogether. No, he decided, it would be better to keep to his original plan when he had boarded the luggage carrier and find out the unknown murderer's destination. Once he knew that and could get a glimpse of his face the rest would be easy.

Just before reaching London Bridge the car swung off the main road taking a turning to the right. They were running parallel with the river now and the street they were traversing was lined on either side with factories and warehouses. After about another half mile John suddenly felt the speed slacken, the car drew into the kerb and came to a halt in front of a pair of high, dilapidated wooden gates. Before it had quite stopped John slipped down to the roadway and laying the now empty oil tin in the gutter concealed himself in the shadow of a doorway close at hand, on the opposite side.

The 'Phantom Slayer' got down from the driving seat and crossed the narrow strip of pavement to the gate. Watching, John saw him fumble in his pocket and after a moment or two there was a rasping, creaking sound and the two heavy gates opened. He pushed them wide, and returning to the car backed it till the long bonnet was pointing at the entrance and then drove it forward. This was John's opportunity! As the big machine ran smoothly through the opening he entered behind it and took up his position under cover of a pile of broken crates that stood just inside. The car went on for two or three yards and then again came to a standstill. He saw the lights go out, heard the slam of a door and then the sound of footsteps coming towards him. The 'Phantom Slayer' passed so near his hiding place that by leaning forward he could have touched him. The man, however, was apparently quite unaware of his presence for he closed the wooden gates and relocked them, pausing to make sure that they were securely fastened, and then went back towards the car.

The place was pitchdark and John could see nothing, but in front of him, in the distance, were a collection of twinkling lights and in the silence he could hear the soft lap of water and concluded that it was a wharf they had come to.

On his right, as his eyes grew accustomed to the darkness, he made out the tall bulk of a building that looked like a factory or warehouse. To his left a forest of girders loomed vaguely out of the gloom, evidently some new building in the course of construction. The 'Phantom Slayer' seemed to have vanished in the deep shadows where the car was standing and although John listened intently he couldn't hear a movement. Probably there was some entrance to the warehouse or whatever it was just there, and the man had gone inside.

John waited for nearly ten minutes and then as nothing happened and the silence remained unbroken he cautiously left his place of concealment and crept forward. Moving stealthily he approached near to the Spange, stopping as he came level with the machine to listen again, but all was still, not a sound came to his straining ears except the noise of the river as it washed against the bank.

He made his way round the car, and found as he had anticipated, that close to it was a door set in the wall of the high building. It was partly open and swung wide on well-oiled hinges under his hand. He entered the dark passage beyond and closed the door behind him. For several seconds he stood in the intense blackness, motionless. He could not see an inch before his eyes and possessing not the least idea of the architectural plan of the place was in some doubt how to proceed. That he was standing in a narrow passage he knew, for by stretching out his arms he could touch the walls with his finger tips, but whether it ran straight ahead or not he couldn't say and he dared not risk a light.

At last he began to advance slowly, feeling his way at every step. It was nervy work and the passage seemed endless, because of the time it took him to cover even a yard, in reality it must have been quite short for suddenly he came to a sharp bend and pausing, held his breath. The passage had twisted to the right and barely four feet away was a half-open door, through which came a faint stream of light. A faint sound greeted his ears — the sound of footsteps on the bare boards. Somewhere beyond that door was the 'Phantom Slayer.'

He moved towards it, inch by inch, carefully testing the floor at every step before throwing his whole weight upon it, for he knew that the creaking of a board would give him away to the man on the other side. He had almost reached the door when he heard a quick movement, the pushing aside of some heavy object, followed by rapidly advancing footsteps. The 'Phantom Slayer' was coming out!

John's keen brain worked quickly, discovery was inevitable, even if he turned and fled his movements would be heard and betray his presence. He pressed himself flat against the wall and waited. The door was jerked open, the light from within flooding the passage and as the 'Phantom Slayer' stepped across the threshold he caught sight of a crouching figure. With a startled cry he fell back and in that moment John acted. Before the man could recover from his surprise he flung himself upon him, bearing him backwards through the doorway with the force of his attack. They fell to the floor with a crash, John uppermost, but it was only a short-lived advantage. His opponent seemed to possess the strength of a tiger and with a supreme effort twisted himself free and throwing his legs over John's body gripped him by the throat.

His steel-like fingers sank deep into John's flesh, and as he increased the pressure the detective felt the blood pounding through his head as though a gigantic steam hammer was working in his brain. With all his strength he tried to loosen that deadly hold, but without avail. His chest was bursting, a red mist floated before his eyes and with a last desperate effort he suddenly shot up his knees. They caught the 'Phantom Slayer' fairly, in the middle of his back, and with a smothered gasp he was thrown over John's head.

Blackmore scrambled to his feet, drawing the air into his lungs with great gulping gasps. His adversary recovered himself quickly and almost before he had time to turn and face him was up again.

They closed and swayed about the narrow passage, each trying his hardest to break away from the other's encircling arm. John had almost succeeded in wrenching his right hand free when his foot slipped and losing his balance he fell backwards, dragging his enemy with him. He felt a sudden, sharp, agonising pain shoot through the back of his head, his senses reeled and with a sensation as though he were falling into a pit of intense blackness he lost consciousness.

* * *

When John recovered his senses his first thought was that his legs and arms had, in some inexplicable fashion, been transformed into lumps of lead. The sub-conscious attempt to move them brought the discovery that it was impossible, and as the mist cleared from his brain he found that the reason lay in the fact that his arms had been securely bound to his sides and that his legs were strapped firmly together.

He was lying on the floor in a large,

bare, unfurnished room. The dim light from a solitary candle stuck on the edge of a packing case cast a feeble patch of radiance in the immediate vicinity, the rest of the place being shrouded in black shadow. As he opened his eyes and took in the scene he saw, also, that seated on a chair beside the light was the 'Phantom Slayer.'

He was still wearing the heavy overcoat and the rubber mask. His head was turned in John's direction and he must have noticed that he had recovered, for presently he spoke in the same muffled tone as before.

'So you've come to your senses, have you?' He rose to his feet and stood over his captive, the flame of the candle reflected in the mica eyeglasses of the mask giving him a peculiar, demoniacal expression. 'I've been wondering during the last ten minutes what to do with you,' he went on, 'and I think I've solved the problem.'

John tried to speak and discovered that he had been effectively gagged.

'You were foolish not to have heeded

my warning,' said the muffled voice evenly, 'and now you'll have to pay the penalty. It was a good disguise, and I must say I never knew who you really were until a few minutes ago. Had I done so I should have taken more pains to assure myself that you had succumbed to the gas at Caesar's Camp. You've done your best to run me to earth and you've succeeded, but it won't do you any good. Falkner succeeded, too, but it didn't do him any good either.' He paused reflectively. 'Shall I tell you how you're going to die?' he continued. 'At first I thought of giving you a dose of gas and dropping your body in the river, but a better plan occurred to me. You would have been found, sooner or later, in the river, I don't suppose you would have been recognisable by then, but still, you would have been found. But I have thought of a scheme by which you will completely disappear for ever, not even your remains will be discovered. Perhaps you noticed that there is a large building in process of being erected next to this warehouse? They are at work on the foundations at present and I was watching them two days ago. It was interesting, but I never thought then that I would be able to turn my casual interest to good account.' He leaned forward slightly. 'D'you know anything about building? The girders supporting the main structure are sunk in shafts twelve to fourteen feet deep, and these shafts are filled in with liquid cement, holding the girders which form the skeleton of the building firmly upright in the centre. There is one shaft left to be filled in first thing in the morning!'

John felt a cold chill creep up his spine as his brain grasped the 'Phantom Slayer's' meaning. Try as he would he could not keep a swift look of horror from leaping to his eyes. The other noticed it evidently, for he nodded slowly.

'I think that you have grasped the idea,' he said with a little throaty chuckle. 'I flatter myself that it's most ingenious. I shall drop you down that shaft bound and gagged as you are. It's too deep and dark for you to be seen at the bottom, and they start work just after dawn. The shoot containing the cement is already fixed into position and the workmen have nothing to do but mix some mortar and let it run in, and you will be buried in the foundations of the building for ever. You ought to thank me for providing you with such a suitable tombstone.'

He spoke in a quiet, conversational tone, and might really have been discussing the weather, but for the note of hatred that every now and again crept into his voice. The cold-bloodedness of the plan made John's fingers itch to get at the man, but he was helpless and unable to move even the fraction of an inch.

He racked his brain to try and think of some way out of this terrible position, but without result. It seemed hopeless. There was, of course, always the possibility that Cartwright might be able to trace the car, but would he arrive in time? Even if he succeeded in finding the warehouse and the probability seemed a slender one, unless he arrived almost immediately he would be too late, for once he, John, was put down the shaft there was not the slightest hope of anyone finding him. If only he could get out of his bonds.

The 'Phantom Slayer' had turned away and was bending over the packing case engaged in examining something under the light of the candle, and John tried again to see if he could loosen the cords that bound his arms and wrists, but the man had done his job well.

The masked man finished his occupation, which appeared to be concerned with some piece of jewellery, and came back to him.

'Well,' he said, looking at his watch, 'you can say goodbye to life, Blackmore. It's time I was off, and I just want to see you snug and comfortable before I go. I suppose you're wondering who I am, eh? Falkner had the advantage of me there, he knew, that's why he died.'

He crossed behind John and the detective heard the rattle of a bolt. He couldn't see what was happening, but from the sudden icy draught that blew upon his face he guessed that the fellow had opened the door. This proved to be the case, for the 'Phantom Slayer' returned and, stooping, put his arms under John's armpits and pulled him along until he reached a narrow opening, through which John caught a glimpse of the river. Leaving him for a moment the man in the mask shut and locked the door, and then half carrying and half dragging him, began to make his way laboriously across what was evidently a disused wharf towards the dark mass of ironwork that reared itself against the night sky and marked the sight of the new building.

By the time he had reached his destination he was panting heavily, it had been no light task getting Blackmore over the uneven ground that lay between, and John himself felt as if he was one mass of bruises.

'There,' grunted the masked man, breathlessly, as he dropped his captive down beside a heap of stones and rubble. 'That's the end of the journey, or I should say, the end of your journey.'

He paused for a brief space to recover his breath, and then, bending down, lifted Blackmore up and staggered over to where a round hole showed blackly against the greyish white of the ground.

From the centre of the shaft rose a slender iron girder, braced with wire to keep it in position, while projecting over the hole was a wooden shoot that sloped upward to a large tank. The 'Phantom Slayer' stopped at the mouth of the pit and deposited his burden so that John's feet hung over the edge.

'Goodbye,' he said. 'I hope you'll be comfortable.'

He gave the detective a shove as he spoke and John slid forward and vanished into the darkness of the shaft!

He landed with a shock that almost made him lose his senses and caused his head to swim. When he had recovered sufficiently from the jolt he looked up.

At first he could see nothing, but after a while succeeded in dimly making out the narrow opening of the well-like hole far above. A single star twinkled faintly in the deep indigo of the sky. The circumference of the shaft was so small there was only just room for his body between the centre girder and the side, and it must have been at least fifteen feet in depth. Even in broad daylight there was little likelihood of anyone seeing him, and long before it was fully light he would be covered by an avalanche of stones and cement.

It was an appalling thought, but he set his teeth and forced himself to await as calmly as he could the terrible death that it seemed nothing but a miracle could avoid!

13

The Man in The Gas Mask

After their brief conversation with the night watchman and the stopping of the car, Cartwright and Kenton had to take a chance that they were going in the right direction when they proceeded down the road towards Wimbledon. They encountered nobody whom they could ask if a car answering the description of the 'Phantom Slayer's' had passed that way. There were several side turnings down any one of which the Spange might have gone, but they considered that it would save time to push on until they came upon a policeman on point duty and learn from him whether a car had gone by. If not, then it would be time enough to try some of the other roads.

Cartwright knew that they were faced with a practically impossible task, since the 'Phantom Slayer' had kept to the main thoroughfares, for if he had branched off down any of the innumerable side streets the probability of tracing him was well-nigh hopeless.

The machine they were travelling in was fast, even if it was on the diminutive side, and almost before they realised it they were running into Wimbledon. They caught sight of the man on point duty outside the station and got the driver to pull up.

'Yes, sir, it went about fifteen minutes ago,' said the constable in answer to Inspector Kenton's question. 'I should have pulled it up when I saw there was someone hanging on the back, but it was going too fast.'

'Which way did it go after it passed you?' snapped the inspector.

'Round that turning,' the policeman pointed. 'Be careful how you go,' he added. 'There's a burst watermain at the corner and the road's flooded. You'll skid if you're not careful.'

'Has any other car turned round here since the Spange?' said Cartwright quickly.

The constable shook his head.

'No,' he replied. 'Only the car you're asking about.'

'Stop at the corner,' said the secretary, as they drove off.

'Why? What's the idea?' growled Kenton.

'The road will be soft there on account of the water,' explained Cartwright, 'and there should be a fairly good impression of the tyre marks of the car we're following.'

'Yes, I see that,' said the inspector, 'but it won't help us very much, we'll only be able to see them just at that spot, the rest of the road is too hard to hold any trace.'

'It may be useful later on,' answered Harry.

He dropped lightly from the little car as it neared the turning and, pulling his torch from his pocket flashed its light on the roadway in front of him. The wheel marks of the Spange were plainly visible in the sodden gravel, the tyres were evidently nearly new, for they were sharp and clear. They were Dunlops, there was no mistaking the circular tread.

Harry was on the point of going back to the car when his attention was attracted to a spot of black grease between the tracks and his forehead wrinkled in a frown, unless the lubricating system was faulty it was unusual for a car to deposit oil while in motion, perhaps one of the pipes was leaking. His heart beat faster with elation as a little further on he came upon another dollop and yet another. Here was a clear clue to follow, providing it continued.

He turned back to the others and related his discovery.

'By Jove!' exclaimed the red-faced man. 'What a great bit of luck, going to make it as easy as a paper chase. I tell you what. I'll drive slowly, well to the side and you can lean over and follow the oil drops and tell me which way to go. How's that?'

'You can drive as fast as you like,' grunted Kenton, 'till we come to any turnings, then we can slow down and look for the oil.'

They set off once more. It was laborious work, for there were many crossroads, and at each they had to stop and reconnoitre the ground for any spots of grease.

Three o'clock was striking when they eventually reached Clapham Junction, but they were still on the track of the car. Cartwright was jubilant. From this point on they received frequent news of the Spange from policemen and coffee stall keepers, for in spite of this their progress was slow and the first faint streaks of light in the eastern sky were heralding the approach of dawn before they arrived at the narrow road by the river in which the warehouse where the 'Phantom Slayer' had driven was situated.

They passed the high wooden gates and continued on for some distance before Cartwright discovered that they had gone too far.

'There's no more sign of any oil marks,' he announced, looking up from where he had been leaning over the side of the car, scouring the road. 'The Spange must have turned off somewhere further back, and as there are no side roads I'd say it had gone through one of these gates.'

The red-faced driver brought his

machine to a halt.

'What are you going to do now?' he asked the secretary.

'We'd better leave the car and walk back up the street,' said Kenton, clambering hurriedly out of the dicky seat, and stretching his cramped limbs. 'It'll be easier to look for traces that way.'

Cartwright agreed, and leaving the car the three of them began to walk slowly along the way they had come. It was a good three hundred yards up the road before they came again to the oil trail.

'Here we are!' cried Harry, who was a short distance in front of the others. 'I've found another grease spot.'

He halted and slashed his torch on the roadway round them.

'H'm, there doesn't seem to be any more,' said Inspector Kenton, looking about after peering at the black circle, 'so the car can't have gone any farther than this.'

An exclamation from their companion drew Cartwright's attention to the red-faced man. He was bending down by the edge of the narrow pavement.

'Look here!' he said excitedly. 'That oil wasn't from a leaking pipe after all, here's the tin it came from.' He pointed to an empty can that lay in the gutter.

'Mr. Blackmore, of course,' said Cartwright. 'He guessed we might try and follow, and left the trail.'

He glanced across the footpath. Opposite him was a pair of wooden gates.

'I shouldn't be surprised if that's where the Spange went,' he continued. 'I'm going to have a look over those gates.' He crossed the pavement and turned to Kenton. 'Give me a leg up,' he said.

The inspector hoisted him on to his broad shoulders and Cartwright peered over the top of the high gateway.

In the dim grey light of the coming dawn he was able to make out faintly the shadowy outline of a large car that stood in the rubbish littered yard beyond.

'I think we've found it,' he whispered to the inspector and dropped lightly to the ground. 'The next thing is to get in.'

Kenton eyed the gate dubiously.

'Well, we can't climb over,' he grunted. 'You might, but I certainly can't.'

'I don't think there'll be any need,' answered Harry.

He was examining the stout padlock that fastened the gate and after a moment's scrutiny took from his pocket a little steel instrument, an invention of his employer's, and inserted it into the keyhole. He twisted a long screw in the handle and presently there was a click and the padlock flew open. The next instant the wooden gates swung wide at his pressure

'Well, I'm jiggered, that was neat!' ejaculated the red-faced man admiringly as they passed through.

Harry held up a warning finger.

'Don't talk,' he muttered. 'The 'Phantom Slayer' must be about somewhere, if that's his car, and we don't want him to hear us.'

He crept over to the machine, and bending down looked at the number plate.

'This is the Spange, right enough,' he whispered. 'Now, the question is, where's Mr. Blackmore?'

He shot a quick glance round. It was getting lighter every moment, and beyond the car he could see a dilapidated wooden staging that had one time obviously been used as a wharf, for the mooring post was visible at the end. It was littered with piles of rotting wood and broken boxes, but there was no sign of Blackmore.

Cartwright walked round the standing car and came upon the door leading to the warehouse. It was ajar, as John had left it when he entered the building some hours previously. Harry pushed it open softly and listened but there was not a sound from the gloomy interior. His uneasiness, which during the excitement of the chase momentarily left him, returned with redoubled force. Somewhere inside was the 'Phantom Slayer.' He must be still there otherwise the car wouldn't have been left, and somewhere also was John Blackmore. But where?

He little guessed that at that moment his employer was calmly facing what he concluded was almost certain death, less than two hundred yards away.

'We'd better go in,' said Kenton, below his breath, and took an automatic pistol from his pocket.

The secretary nodded and was about to step gently across the threshold when suddenly the silence was burst by a shot. It seemed to come from the side of the building that faced the river and was followed by a smothered cry.

In a trice Cartwright had spun round, and with Kenton panting at his heels went racing towards the corner of the warehouse. As he turned it, the noise of tramping feet somewhere above caused him to look up quickly and the sight that met his gaze brought him sharply to a stop.

Half way up the side of the building was a wooden ledge supported on rusty chains and projected out over the river, and on this platform, locked together and swaying this way and that, were the figures of two men, struggling violently. Back and forth they staggered, fighting desperately, and every moment getting nearer to the unprotected edge of the curious drawbridge.

'Look!' breathed Harry, grasping the inspector by the arm, and even as he spoke the two figures reeled to the edge of the platform, overbalanced and fell.

They struck the edge of the wharf with a horrible thud and rebounding, rolled off into the river with a splash.

Cartwright recovered himself and tore to the spot, his heart in his mouth, for he was convinced that one of them was Blackmore. There was nothing to be seen as he looked down except a series of ever widening ripples in the water, and without hesitation he slipped off his coat and dived into the river.

He came to the surface and shook the water from his eyes. Something bumped against him and he saw a dark form floating near. It was shallow by the muddy bank and clinging to a pile he reached forward and dragged the limp figure on to the shore. One glance satisfied him that it was not his employer, for the man's face was covered by a rubber mask, and he repressed a shudder as he saw that the back of the head was battered to pulp. He hurriedly pulled the thing that had once been a man on to a strip of ooze and started to search for the other, with a cold sensation round his heart. He thought that there would be no doubt that it was John Blackmore.

While he was so engaged, Kenton and his companion, seeing what was happening, started laboriously to climb down towards him from the top of the wharf.

It was some time before Cartwright located the second man, but he found him at last, and with the assistance of Kenton hauled him up beside the man in the mask. His gasp of relief was audible when he caught sight of the face that was not the one he had hoped and yet dreaded to see. The man was a perfect stranger to the secretary, but apparently not to Kenton, for that worthy, bending over the body uttered an exclamation.

'Great Scott!' he ejaculated, 'Abe Steen!'

'Do you know him?' said Cartwright.

'I should say I do,' replied Kenton. 'He's one of the cleverest crooks in London, and Lew Steen, the first victim of the 'Phantom Slayer' was his brother.'

Cartwright drew a long breath.

'Lew Steen's brother, eh?' He looked at the still form, a sudden light breaking in on his mind. 'I think I see.'

Kenton was stooping above the man in the mask.

'This must be the 'Phantom Slayer' himself,' he said. 'He's received a terrible injury, and appears to be stone dead. We might as well have a look at the beauty.'

He fumbled at the fastenings of the rubber gas mask and gently took it off. The next instant he staggered up with a cry.

'Merciful God, look!' he cried, and Cartwright looking in speechless amazement saw the face of George Mellish, star reporter on the *Megaphone!*

14

Steen's Story

He quickly recovered from his first shock of amazement.

'Fancy it being Mellish,' he muttered. 'I can scarcely believe it.'

'I don't think there's much doubt,' grunted Kenton, 'but I must admit that I was never more surprised in my life.' He turned his attention to Steen. 'This fellow's still alive,' he went on, after a short examination. 'We ought to get him away from here as soon as possible and fetch a doctor, he's breathing, but he seems pretty far gone, he may be suffering from some internal injury.'

Cartwright looked doubtfully at the front of the wharf.

'You're right,' he agreed. 'But I don't see how we're going to get up there. It's easy enough to climb alone but — '

The red-faced man who had been

watching in silence broke in:

'I saw a ladder round the side of the warehouse,' he remarked. 'Shall I go and get it?'

'That's what we want,' said Kenton. 'If you can drop it down to us, and stay up above to receive this chap as I bring him up we can manage it.'

The other nodded and began to climb up the wharf, and in a moment or two had hauled himself over the edge.

'I can't understand what's become of Mr. Blackmore,' said Cartwright, when they were alone, his forehead puckered in an uneasy frown. 'Where the dickens can he be?'

'Perhaps after he traced Mellish to this place he went off to find the nearest police station,' suggested Kenton.

The secretary shook his head.

'He wouldn't do that,' he said. 'He wouldn't lose sight of Mellish once he got as far as this, in case the man escaped while he was away.'

The inspector pursed his rather thin lips.

'That's true,' he admitted. 'I hope

nothing's happened to him. We'd better search the warehouse as soon as we've got Steen to a more comfortable spot.'

'Here you are,' said a voice from above, and then the end of a ladder appeared over the edge of the wall.

Cartwright grasped it and placed it into position, holding it steady while Kenton picked up the injured crook and started to ascend gingerly. The red-faced man leaned over as he neared the top and stretching out his arms took his burden from him. A second later Cartwright sprang lightly up the ladder in the inspector's wake.

'We can leave Mellish for the moment,' he said as they carried Steen into the warehouse. 'The most important thing at present is to find out what has happened to Mr. Blackmore.'

They made the man as comfortable as possible on a bed of old sacks, that they discovered in one of the lower rooms, and Kenton sent their companion off to the nearest police station with a message for the divisional inspector in charge.

It was daylight now and when he had

departed on his errand they proceeded to make a close search of the building. In the upstairs rooms, from which the platform projected over the river they discovered a jeweller's bench and a lapidary's wheel. On a chair beside the bench was a bag, half full of jewellery that had evidently been taken from a small, box-like receptacle in the floor, for a section of one of the boards had been removed, disclosing a shallow cavity. This, too, contained jewellery in all shapes and forms, necklaces, brooches, pendants, rings, a wonderful collection of precious stones, set and unset.

'Great Scott!' cried Kenton as he looked at them, 'these are the proceeds of most of the great robberies during the past eight months.'

'Never mind them for the moment,' said Cartwright, impatiently. 'They'll keep.'

Nevertheless, in spite of the secretary's protest, the inspector scooped them up in a bag and snapping it shut carried it with him when they continued the search.

They explored every inch of the place,

from the roof to the basement, but there was not a sign of Blackmore.

'He's certainly not here,' said Kenton, when he and Cartwright returned into the room where they had left Steen.

'I don't like the look of it at all,' declared the secretary. 'The river's handy and if Mellish discovered he had been followed he might — '

He broke off, leaving the sentence unfinished, staring at the floor, and then suddenly, just as Kenton had opened his mouth to reply he stooped eagerly forward and peered at the dusty boards.

'What is it?' asked the Scotland Yard man quickly.

'Something heavy has been dragged along here,' said Cartwright. 'Look here, you can see the traces plainly in the dust.'

'Yes, you're right,' said the inspector, following the direction of his pointing finger. 'Those two parallel lines look uncommonly like heel marks, too.'

Harry didn't answer, he was busy following the track with his eyes. It led to a narrow door in the wall and crossing over he tried the latch. It was locked, but the woodwork was old and when Kenton applied his brawny shoulders with the whole weight of his body behind, the screws tore from the rotting planks, the door burst open.

They stepped across the threshold and found themselves once more on the wharf, the marks were still visible but the place was covered in half an inch of grime. Cartwright, with the inspector at his heels, followed them across to a low wall of stone, behind which they could see a forest of iron. Evidently there was a building of some sort in the course of construction on the other side. Cartwright vaulted over the wall and looked round him. Scattered all about were piles of stones and bricks, troughs for mixing mortar, picks and shovels and the preparations that usually accompany the erection of a new structure.

Little groups of workmen had already arrived and were taking off their coats preparatory to starting the day's work. Cartwright searched the ground at his feet, surely the 'Phantom Slayer' hadn't brought his employer here? What reason could he have for doing so? But there was the trail, more pronounced than ever in the grey and white cement dust that covered everything.

The secretary advanced, his eyes on the ground, and presently a shout caused him to look up.

'Hi?' cried a voice. 'What do you want?'

A tall, thick-set man was approaching, evidently a foreman, but Cartwright took no heed of him, in fact after the first shout that caused him to raise his head he never even heard him. His gaze was fixed on a group of men who surrounded a raised trough, the end projected over a hole in the ground and they were in the act of pulling up a kind of sluice gate. Cartwright had seen a similar apparatus before and knew that the raising of the sluice would result in a rush of liquid cement and stone, and like a flash, the possibility of John Blackmore's where-abouts entered his brain.

'Stop!' he cried hoarsely, rushing forward to the well-like aperture.

The man who was about to pull the lever that worked the sluice gates paused, startled, as Harry flung himself full length, and peered into the black depths of the shaft. He could see nothing, and stretched out his hand to Kenton.

'Give me your torch.'

The inspector had grasped his meaning, and with a hand that trembled in excitement he gave him the flash lamp. Cartwright sent a beam of white light streaming to the bottom of the pit, and instantly revealed a figure that stood propped against the girder.

'It's Mr. Blackmore,' he cried brokenly as he saw the pallid upturned face. 'I don't know whether he's alive or — or dead, but he's here and we must get him out.'

Kenton explained to the questioning and amazed foreman and willing hands set to work immediately to rescue John Blackmore from the depths of the shaft, that might easily have been his grave.

* * *

It was half an hour later and Blackmore, looking pale and haggard, but feeling, except for a headache, little the worse after his horrible experience, was standing by the side of the rough couch of sacks on which Kenton had placed the injured Steen.

The divisional surgeon had arrived and was looking gravely down at the recumbent figure of the crook, who had recovered consciousness and was moaning fitfully. The body of George Mellish had been brought from the river bank and was lying in a corner covered by a tarpaulin, and grouped behind Blackmore and the the doctor were Cartwright, Inspector Kenton, and the red-faced man who had helped them in tracking down the car. By themselves, a little way off, stood an inspector in the uniform of the City Police and a constable.

'I suppose there's no hope of his recovering, poor fellow?' said John, addressing the doctor.

The divisional surgeon shook his head.

'Not the slightest,' he replied. 'His back's broken. He may live twenty-four hours, he may live longer, there's no telling in these cases, but I'm afraid he can't possibly recover.'

They had spoken in low tones, but the man must have heard for he turned his head towards them and looked at John.

'Going to die, am I?' he whispered huskily. 'Well, there are one or two things I'd like to say before I go.' He paused and winced as a spasm of pain racked him. 'Mellish is dead, isn't he? I'm glad of that. I shouldn't have died happy if he'd been alive,' he continued. 'I tried to get him before; you nearly copped me when I was running away from his flat.'

'So you were the man,' said John gently.

'Yes, I was the man,' answered Steen. 'Two of us had banded together to get the 'Phantom Slayer,' myself and another fellow, partly for revenge because he killed my brother, Lew, and partly because we thought that if we could find him we might possibly get hold of the stuff he'd stolen. For weeks we searched, and at last our suspicions were narrowed down to one man, who called himself Arthur Rees. We knew that he was a crook, and by accident we found out that he was disguised; another peculiar thing about him was that he used to disappear from all his regular haunts at frequent intervals, and nobody seemed to know what his particular graft was, although he always had plenty of money. We managed to trail him one day and discovered that his real name was Mellish, and that he lived in a flat, Evesham Mansions. He had a job as a newspaper reporter on the *Megaphone.'*

Steen stopped and passed his tongue over his dry lips.

'Of course, we weren't certain that he was the 'Phantom Slayer' even then,' he went on, after a pause. 'He might quite easily have been disguised for purposes of his own in connection with the paper, but we knew that he was an old lag, and it seemed suspicious. We kept a close watch on him, taking it in turns, and one night I succeeded in following him down here. I watched him go into his warehouse and after a short interval saw a large car drive up. I had my motorcycle with me so I was able to keep on his track. I trailed him to a lonely road crossing Wimbledon Common. It was the night Gold was killed, and I saw that happen. We had proof now, and on the following night we decided to force Mellish to tell us where he kept the stolen stuff. We went to the flat in Evesham Mansions and it was arranged that one of us should keep watch outside while I broke in and got the information we needed. I climbed the fire escape and entered Mellish's flat by the bedroom window. I could hear him moving in the sitting room and peered through the open door. He was bending down close to the wall near the fireplace, before he could move I was on him. I struck him once on the back of the head with my life preserver and down he went without a sound. I bound and gagged him and carried him into the bedroom. I watched until he had recovered consciousness then questioned him about the whereabouts of the jewellery. I threatened to kill him unless he told me. I intended to kill him, anyway, but I didn't let him know that. He didn't know I was Lew's brother, because I was wearing a handkerchief over my face, and he was scared to death, I could see that by his eyes. I think I should have got the information I wanted then only your arrival at the next door flat frightened me. I didn't know it was you, then, of course, because I didn't know anything about the murder. There seemed to be something happening because I could hear the sound of several people on the stairs and a door kept opening and shutting. I was going to escape by the way I had come, by the fire escape, but I heard somebody moving about in the yard below and was afraid of being caught and questioned. I switched out the light in the bedroom, left Mellish, and went into the hall. I listened until everything was, as I thought, quiet and then opened the door with the intention of creeping down the stairs and getting away. When I saw you I got a panic and made a dash for it.'

He stopped to recover his breath and John waited in silence for him to continue.

'There's very little more,' he went on after a short interval. 'Alden had disappeared. I suppose he had seen you arrive and recognised you. I read about the murder in the papers the next day, and from then until now I've kept a close watch upon Mellish. I tried to get him when he visited you, but it's difficult to aim straight from a motorcycle at the speed I was going.'

A spasm of pain shook him and he bit his lip, while the perspiration broke out on his forehead.

'You know nearly all the rest,' he continued almost immediately. 'I'd come to the conclusion that he had hidden the stones and stuff in the warehouse, somewhere. Although I'd spent several nights, when I knew that he was safely at home, I couldn't find it. I was watching Mellish last night but he gave me the slip. I missed him in a traffic hold-up and went home, but after I'd had supper I thought I'd come down here and make another search. I knew he was here when I arrived because I saw the car, but I didn't care because I meant to finish matters. He was upstairs, packing a small bag with jewellery, which he was taking from a hiding place in the floor. It was my chance. I drew a revolver and crept up behind him. It was my intention to shoot him then and there but just as my fingers pressed the trigger a board creaked under my weight and he swung round. The bullet went wide and he closed with me. I'm glad he's dead, and I'm glad I was responsible for it!'

The exertion of speaking had been too much for him, and as he finished he closed his eyes, his breath hissing through his suddenly clenched teeth in short pants.

The divisional surgeon bent down quickly and at the same moment Abe Steen gave a convulsive shudder. His mouth opened as though he were about to speak but no word came, his hands clutched at the rough sacking that covered him until his knuckles gleamed white, then suddenly he relaxed, there was a little choking rattle in his throat and he lay still.

The doctor stooped lower and touched the half-closed eyes, then he straightened up.

'It's all over,' he said in a low tone, and gently drew one of the sacks over the white face.

The last words were spoken in John Blackmore's study in Mecklinburg Square, whence they had returned after the death of Steen.

'I expect you'll find all the jewellery that has been stolen practically intact,' said John, nodding his head in the direction of the bag that Kenton had religiously clung to and brought with him.

'Yes, I think it's nearly all there,' asserted the inspector. 'Of course, I can't tell until I've compared it with the list at the Yard.'

'I wonder why Mellish made no effort to dispose of it,' remarked Cartwright, pouring out another cup of coffee.

'I think it was his intention to wait until he had left the country,' answered John. 'It would have been difficult to get rid of it here, for every fence would have been on the look-out, and directly he tried to sell to any one of them, he would have given away the fact that he was the 'Phantom Slayer,' and you mustn't forget that every criminal in London was as keen to get him as we were.'

'It seems a pity that a fellow like Mellish should have gone crook,' said Kenton. 'He must have been earning a jolly good salary from the *Megaphone*.'

'He had a criminal kink,' replied John. 'You see, he'd already served a sentence earlier in his life as Arthur Rees, which I've no doubt is his real name. There are people who would rather make sixpence by foul means than earn it by fair, Mellish was one of them. Add to that the fact that he was utterly without a conscience of any kind and the result is a foregone conclusion.'

'How do you think he knew that Falkner was going to ring you up?' said Harry after a short silence.

'Now that we know that Mellish was the 'Phantom Slayer,'' answered John, 'the explanation, I think, is a simple one. Falkner's phone was on a table close to the wall which divides the two flats. The wall was a thin one, as we know, and it would have been quite easy for Mellish in his sitting room to have heard Falkner speaking. Directly he heard sufficient to let him know what was happening he had only to slip along to the landing and cut the wire.'

'Do you suppose he knew who Falkner really was?' grunted Kenton.

John shook his head.

'No, I don't think he did until then,' he replied. 'If he had known earlier he would have guessed why Falkner had taken the flat next door, and made an attempt to kill him before. The whole thing was obviously done on the spur of the moment, otherwise he would never have gone to work so clumsily. It was purely by chance that Steen chose that night to break in. If he hadn't done so and left Mellish bound and gagged, suspicion would have pointed to him from the start. It was Steen's presence in the flat that scared Mellish; no doubt he would have plugged the hole in the wall after killing Falkner, and arranged matters to look as if Falkner's flat had been broken into. Probably he would have put the gas pistol beside the body, certainly he would never have left things as they were, but the unexpected arrival of Steen prevented him doing anything.'

'But why didn't he break into Falkner's flat in the first place?' he asked. 'Why bore the hole at all?'

'Obviously,' said John, 'because there was no time to do anything else. Falkner must have been aware that the line was cut immediately, and if Mellish had tried to break in by the front door there's a strong probability that Falkner would have got out by the fire escape and given the alarm. On the other hand, if Mellish had broken in by the back, Falkner would have left by the front. He took the only chance, and bored the hole, making sufficient noise to attract Falkner's attention and bring him over to see what was taking place. The rest was simple.'

'I'd like to know how Falkner got on his track in the first place,' said Kenton, helping himself to one of John's cigars.

'That we shall never find out for certain,' answered Blackmore, 'but I think the probability is that Falkner, while searching for a clue to the 'Phantom Slayer's' identity amongst some of the crime haunts of London saw Mellish in his capacity of Rees, recognised him in spite of his disguise, and followed him to Evesham Mansions.'

'And why take the flat next door?' asked Kenton.

'Well, obviously,' replied John. 'Even if Falkner had pierced Mellish's disguise, it wouldn't have given him any definite proof that he was really the 'Phantom Slayer.' He might have had his suspicions but he would naturally want to turn them into certainties before making any statement, and by taking the flat next door to the man he suspected he provided himself with a very excellent point of vantage from which to keep an eye on Mellish's movements.'

'Well, it's all over now,' said Kenton. 'And I must take these jewels along to the Yard. What are you going to do?'

John Blackmore stretched himself with a yawn.

'I'm going to bed,' he said with a smile, 'and I should recommend, Kenton, that at the first opportunity you do the same!'

THE END

We do hope that you have enjoyed reading this large print book.

Did you know that all of our titles are available for purchase?

We publish a wide range of high quality large print books including:
Romances, Mysteries, Classics
General Fiction
Non Fiction and Westerns

Special interest titles available in large print are:
The Little Oxford Dictionary
Music Book, Song Book
Hymn Book, Service Book

Also available from us courtesy of Oxford University Press:
Young Readers' Dictionary
(large print edition)
Young Readers' Thesaurus
(large print edition)

For further information or a free brochure, please contact us at:
Ulverscroft Large Print Books Ltd.,
The Green, Bradgate Road, Anstey,
Leicester, LE7 7FU, England.
Tel: (00 44) 0116 236 4325
Fax: (00 44) 0116 234 0205

Dr. Brutus Lloyd was no more than four feet ten inches tall, an amazingly gnome-like man. The most surprising thing about him was his deep bass voice. A brilliant scientist and criminologist, his unorthodox methods caused consternation to Inspector Branson of the New York City Police when: an accident caused a mining engineer to see into 'another world'; four scientists were murdered for their collective brainpower, and when dinosaurs were seen on the outskirts of a village . . .

THE MENACE OF LI-SIN

Nigel Vane

When Doctor James Hartley meets up with the son of an old friend, he discovers that young Jack Mallory is in fear of his life. Having stolen the sacred Black Idol from the Temple of Tsao-Sun in China, he is being followed by emissaries of the Temple priests. Mallory is advised by Hartley to return the idol, but then it's stolen, sparking a series of murders. Both their lives, and those of their families and friends, are in danger . . .

THE AVENGERS

Derwent Steele

The criminal mastermind known only as 'Simon Boyle' has amassed a vast fortune defrauding banks. Scotland Yard, unable to identify and apprehend him, is forced to call in private detective John Blackmore. Blackmore's investigations lead to Boyle's arrest — but not before he brutally murders the detective's informant. After his trial, still hiding his real identity, Boyle faces execution. But his vow, that he will be avenged, threatens that Blackmore and those responsible for his death will be killed . . .